SHANTANU JAIN

Notion Press

Old No. 38, New No. 6
McNichols Road, Chetpet
Chennai - 600 031

First Published by Notion Press 2019
Copyright © Shantanu Jain 2019
All Rights Reserved.

ISBN 978-1-64587-155-2

Disclaimer

This is a work of fiction. Names, characters, places and incidents are either the product of the author's imagination or are used fictitiously, and any resemblance to any actual person, living or dead, events or locales is entirely coincidental.

Dedicated to my love, our dearest son,
parents and family.

Contents

Part II

Part III

Prologue

Present

In our office, the team party was long overdue. Today was the day we had finally planned for it. The venue was decided, at the Farmaish Pub situated in Viman Nagar, Pune. Though it was small, its beautiful interior made it an attractive venue, ideally suited for a small gathering. While we were waiting for all the team members to arrive, Prerana, who was the youngest and the tallest in our team, suggested playing 'Truth or Dare'.

"Now what is that, Prerana?"

"Ah, it's a very nice game. To play it, you need to spin a bottle. Once the bottle stops spinning, whoever it points to must answer a question with the truth or perform a dare." We all agreed to play the game. "Okay, let's start," said Prerana.

The bottle started spinning. Finally it stopped, pointing at our manager, Shikha, with the other end pointing towards me. I asked, "Was yours a love marriage or was it arranged? And if love, how did you meet him?"

"I am not sure what you would call it. We were best friends, but we never thought of ourselves in that way. Our parents were looking for partners for us, but all the same, we did not like anyone. Whenever we both met up, we discussed what kind of *Champu* or *Champi* we had found. Finally, it was our parents who noticed us. Since our parents were family friends as well, they suggested we marry each other as we were firm friends. That is how we ended up marrying each other." Again, the spinning started and at last, the bottle top pointed at me with the other end at Prerana's side. It seemed like a gun, pointed at me, which can fire at any moment.

Prerana fired, "Did you ever have an extramarital affair in your life? If yes, did it mean you reached a point where both of you decided to end your marriage and part ways, but somehow the situation was instead saved?"

"That's a tricky question. There is quite a long story behind it, which I am not sure you would like to hear."

"So you have some story to tell us. Carry on, we are listening.," Prerana said excitedly. "Remember now that you must dare to tell the truth."

"If that is your wish then I will begin. In our society, affairs before marriage are still divine, but after marriage, it is always considered a sin, no matter if you fall in love with yourself. Every life has a story hidden in it, no matter how boring it may appear. Although my life too is a bit boring, I do have a story. Let me start with that fateful cold night, when I was stuck shivering on the roof, lying on a cot."

Part 1

1

Friends, I Need Help and Support

Almost Five Years Back

It was the last day of the year. Since morning, I had not been feeling well, and so I left the office early. It's not that my body was letting me down. It was just that I was mentally exhausted by the annoying questions that preoccupied my thoughts and to which I did not have any answers. I was feeling drained and sleepy, as if I had not slept for many days.

When I reached home, I found the door locked. Somehow, this eerie feeling hit me. The first question that came into my mind was, "Has she really gone?" I tried to remain composed and comforted myself with the thought, "No, my dear wife can't leave me like this without hearing me out." I thought that she might have gone somewhere nearby. So I waited for another half an hour. But nothing happened; neither did she come nor was there any news about her. There was only me, wrapped in loneliness and silence, feeling extremely hollow inside.

To my horror and disbelief, I found I was not even able to stand up. I needed the support of the staircase railing. Half-heartedly and slowly, I climbed up the stairs and went to the roof. I found a cot there, and lay down upon it. The sky was filled with scattered little clouds like a net hanging in the air. Amid the clouds, little stars were twinkling intermittently, confined behind the net.It was how my life waslike, limited to bars of unhappiness. Soon, I was trapped in a storm of thoughts that completely clogged my mind.

The last few days had been a tough time for me; the more I wanted to get rid of this feeling, the more it seeped deeply into my life. Even in my dreams, it was literally haunting me. I believed that the only way to gain some respite from it was to accept the truth, to confess publicly that:

"I Was in Love"

Yes, I was in love erroneously, sincerely and even regretfully. Every day brought a new meaning and unravelled a new truth about it, of which I had been utterly unaware until now. Every moment of my life had been a swing between what was right and what was wrong, only in the name of practicality, which in fact was a myth.

Restless mornings, sleepless nights, burdensome mornings and soulless evenings – half of my life had gone by wondering whether this was what happened when one was in love. If yes, then why hadn't I felt it before? Why did I feel it at that time? It could be that the life we are living, the fast pace of the world around us and the struggle to achieve worldly pleasures insulate us from our inner self which lies just around our heart.

I didn't want to fall prey to this now. I was scared of this swamp. Unfortunately, the more I wanted to get out of this, the more I got dragged into it. I really didn't know what to do. I didn't want to live in this mirage day in and day out, so I started to share my thoughts in the virtual world.

So let me quickly tell you about her before the rumours and wild guesses start flying thick and fast. I first met her almost ten years back at my cousin's wedding. Now once again, she had reappeared in my life, trapping me between the devil and the deep blue sea. On the one hand there was my practical wife and on the other, my love in whose thoughts I was badly stuck.

She was beautiful, lovely and so charming that when I first saw her, I was utterly bowled over. It was love at first sight. Though it was almost ten years ago, the memory of my first sight of her was so fresh and vivid that it seemed to be happening right in front of me even now.

She was beautifully attired in a sky-blue sari. Her long flowing hair fell down from her shoulders to her waist like a dark cloud. She seemed a little hesitant, but her huge dark blue eyes were full of life and attentive like a deer. She was walking swiftly with a strange, mysterious smile on her beautiful lips. She was accompanied by her younger sister, who was also dressed very attractively in a white top, jeans and a long jacket.

My cousin introduced me to her as her best friend, Aaisha. Then and there I decided that I would make her my best friend too. With some chatting and a bit of flirting, the night was over in no time. I said goodbye to her, praying

I would meet her again. However, my efforts to make her a good friend went in vain because we could not even exchange phone numbers. Her face was profoundly carved into my heart so that it was impossible to forget her, but I had little choice as I had to leave the next day for Mumbai - my *karmsthali,* where I had a job and was living with six other roommates who belonged to different states in India.

India is known for its diverse culture and despite our cultural differences, we are united. Similarly, though we belonged to different cultures, we lived like a family in our Andheri flat. Rajiv and Kamal were from West Bengal, Satya from Bihar, Abhishek from Maharashtra, Ashish from Uttar Pradesh and Rathi Sahib from Tamil Nadu. I hailed from Rajasthan. Since it was our first job in Mumbai, five of us had come together because we worked in same office; Ashish and Rathi Sahib joined us because of Satya, as they were his referrals.

At that time, I did not know if it was love or just an attraction. I knew that she was not going to meet me again. There was no way that I could get in touch with her. So I just let such ideas go. I convinced myself that it was the end of a small story. But this story was not going to end so early, and it happened again, very soon after.

2

A Storm Had Just Started Brewing...

I was working in one of the largest private insurance companies in Mumbai. As soon as I reached the city, my life became very busy with long working hours and chaotic traffic, but somewhere, something was amiss. Despite all the pressures of a hectic job, I just could not concentrate on anything. It was as if I was slipping into a trance, gazing at particular objects for an extended period yet somehow managing to hide it from everyone around me.

I had always wondered what exactly happens when one is in love. As may be heard everywhere, "How can somebody think of just one person, day in and day out?" But now, I began to understand the matter more. I still could not believe that this could happen to me because I thought love and such silly things were the creation of films, featuring mythical events, actors dancing around trees, songs at the drop of a hat, macho fighting and all the usual melodrama. It was as if love and such things were not meant for me.

Many times I thought about discussing this with someone. There could not have been a better person than Satya, who was the most supportive and helpful guy amongst us. He was one of my roommates. He was the most experienced one amongst us in matters of love and romance. We always used to pull his leg about this, but I still could not muster enough courage to speak with him about it. I felt very uncomfortable talking about such things. I was also scared to imagine what these guys would get up to once they knew about it. I did try to get rid of the feeling, but the more I wanted to avoid it, the more it started to follow me.

Everything suddenly changed for me. Romance was in the air. I could feel it even with my eyes closed. It was so beautiful, so electrifying that I get goose bumps even as I write this now. For the first time, I felt that life exists in reality in this beautiful world.

Be it the unstoppable rain of Mumbai when the crickets start chanting to express their love to the lovely showers during those dark nights. Be it the stinking, extensive open drain behind the office situated in Malad, which flows like a river in the rainy season or all those unnoticed beautiful small butterflies, flying around the park in front of my building. Be it the tidal waves of the Hind Sea roaring like, "Mumbai, we are coming to kiss you." Be it all those fireflies who glitter in the night as though they are all telling the same story - the feeling of love turned all those aspects of nature into a mysterious wonderland where every moment seemed like bliss.

For the first time I felt Mayavi Nagri (Mumbai) alive and beautiful, all those small moments it encompassed, which we tend to ignore in the name of the myth of success, which is never real. We keep chasing it, and it never ends. It is like a mirage in the desert.

Whenever I saw couples wandering around at a movie theatre or CCD, an office canteen, or one of those dating spotsin Mumbai like Bandra Bandstand, Nariman Point, I always imagined that she was with me, by my side. The more I tried to get away from her, the closer I became to her.

An atheist converted to a believer. I started believing in every monument where God is thought to exist, in statues or in any other form. I would pray whenever I got a chance, and I would not miss doing so. God is so great that you always get a second chance to live again. I understood then why God does not give you a second chance if you kill yourself. If you continue to live and fight, then hope always exists - but after death, nothing exists - only infinity.

If God puts you in a difficult situation, he always shows you some way to emerge from it. This time, he sent me Rajiv as his messenger. Rajiv was the most unpredictable and moody family member in Mumbai, with a rapidly receding hairline that made him obsessively protective about his few remaining strands of hair. But he was also the wisest, most understanding and unflappable character in challenging situations.

Rajiv caught me red-handed when I was stuck on the same page of 'The Fountainhead' byAyn Rand for hours. The book was in my hand, but my mind and my whole self was drowning in her eyes. So when he insisted, I had to tell him my story about her.

"So this is the problem. Every problem has a solution, but first, it needs to be accepted wholeheartedly." Before I could react, it was declared that I was in love in a place where seven characters were always looking for such *masala* like bloodhounds. Afterwards, it was like a storm had hit our place. It felt like everything was flowing into it and nothing could be heard in that. I was the only victim of that storm. Every thought of mine was torn apart. Finally, the storm ended with the remark, "We've got another Satya now."

But how was I going to get help? This in itself was a complete mystery to me.

3

I Kept on Waiting, Waiting and Waiting...

After the storm passed, things settled down a bit. Everybody felt the need for a hot cup of tea, but none of us could be bothered to make it at midnight. I had to finally put up my hand to volunteer to do it because, after midnight, I didn't have the luxury of asking Babloo to prepare it for us. Babloo was our servant and stayed with us. Rather than treating him as a servant, we always treated him as our younger brother. He got all the luxuries, and it might be said, sometimes enjoying things that were not even available to us. The entire semi-furnished flat belonged to him alone when we left for the office each day, and he lived there like a king.

I always find tea to be a perfect stress reliever. It was almost an unwritten rule for me to prepare the midnight tea for everyone. Every time I made tea at weird hours of the night, somehow, whether it was by force or by choice, everybody wanted to have it. I used to love those moments and had taken responsibility for it. After all, I used to prepare perfect tea. If I had not done accounting, then my career would have definitely ended up at the tea stall. In fact, my father, had already bought a kiosk in front of his office. I could not see a better business idea than that.

Anyway, I left all of them in the room to brainstorm and find the perfect solution to my strange problem. It was strange because I didn't know much about her except for her name and that she was living in Jaipur doing the final year of her MBA, and also that I did not dare to call my cousin for her number. I didn't even remember the name of her college so that I could try to reach her using that. A lot of plans were floated around that night, but all were discarded because none of them could agree on any one idea.

In the kitchen, I saw Babloo pretending that he was fast asleep, but I could see the light of his mobile and hear him whispering beneath his blanket. On another day, I would have walloped him, but that day I didn't disturb him. I threw open the window of the kitchen. And as I opened it, a cool breeze suddenly hit me. It took me to a different world where angels existed behind the stars and the moon. For the first time, I noticed a full moon night in Mumbai. I saw her smiling face bathed in the light. It was as if she was teasing me, saying, "Find out if you love me," and I was looking at her helplessly. I didn't know what I felt in those moments; I was so full of emotions that suddenly I felt tears rolling down my cheeks.

I don't know how long I stood there, but suddenly my thoughts were interrupted by Abhishek's irritating voice that brought me back to the real world. "Shants, one option is that you go to Jaipur and sing songs on the roads in front of every MBA college. Hopefully, you will find her like it happens in a Bollywood movie." Abhishek was the most cunning of all of us, always preoccupied with naughty thoughts and pestering you until you told him everything. He was the reason why we gorged on outside food despite having all the facilities at our place including a cook as good as Babloo. He was very fussy about his own food, wanting it without garlic and onion, which was irritating for all of us and very annoying for Babloo as sometimes he had to cook twice.

Finally, when I brought in the tray loaded with cups of hot tea, Rajiv suggested, "Now the only option we are left with is to get help from social networking sites." This was the solution we all agreed on, and a resolution was passed. "Shants, have you ever cared to leave your Ayn Rand world and interact with people. Do you have an account on Orkut?" Rajiv questioned me and ordered Ashish to open an Orkut account for me. He knew I didn't have one as I hardly spent any time in the virtual world. I always lost myself in a novel in my leisure time. "Hope *Bhabhi Ji* is not like him," Abhishek commented. I knew his devious mind could not remain silent. Every topic had to end with his artful comments.

Ashish drafted two individual messages on my Orkut account. One for her, and another for her sister as a backup, and it was sent to everyone who had a similar name. Though her sister was an IT engineering student, we were sure that she could not be missing from the virtual world, yet we were not able to locate her profile from her picture. Ashish was the most intelligent, with a strong academic background, and the youngest guy among us, with a skinny build and a broad forehead.

After the messages were sent, we waited for hours, days and then weeks. Reminders were mailed, and some of them accepted my friend request, probably either impressed by the tone of the message or just to add another number to their ever-growing friend's list; however, neither she nor her sister appeared along the way. As the days passed, all hope began to dwindle. My heart started sinking inside slowly and gradually, but I kept waiting, waiting and waiting.

4

Finally I Saw a Ray of Hope...

The message read, "I believe in honesty, and instead of trying to beat around the bush, I want to say that the moment I saw you, I was bowled over and you may either call it attraction or love, but I want to talk to you. So if you are the same girl who met me at my cousin Alka's wedding, please write back to me."

As I lay on the cot, I was brought back to the present from those glorious days by the vicious bite of some insect. This day was not too different from that day when I was waiting for her response, and now I was waiting for my wife who left me on discovering my love. I know that what I did was wrong on my part. I should have apologized to her but honestly, I had not broken her faith and trust and she should not have left me like this, without even giving me a chance to explain myself. I know yesterday evening was catastrophic for us. We both want to forget this, which was the worst evening of our lives until now.

I know that our relationship is not so weak that it will break just because of this issue. Deep within my heart, I know that she will come back, seeking answers to her questions. After all, marriage is based on the pillars of trust and understanding, which we both agreed to from the time of the seven oaths, which as the saying goes, applies to seven births. One storm surely cannot destroy those pillars so that the entire edifice collapses, though at times it does shake them.

By now all the scattered clouds had merged together. They formed a thick layer completely engulfing the stars and the beautiful moon, making the night much darker and grimmer. To make matters worse, for some reason the streetlights failed to turn on that day. A cold, freezing winter wind started blowing and sent a chilling shiver down my spine. I could not even stand up. As the wind picked up, a strange hissing arose from the trees around my place, owing to the movement of the leaves, and made it a terrifying night. Soon, even fog set in and engulfed everything, making the lone distant streetlight give up its fight against nature appearing in its scariest avatar. I didn't know whether it was just the beginning of the war or whether it was going to end very soon.

Suddenly I saw a flash of light and felt like something was happening downstairs. I recovered my strength and rushed down, but I could not find anything. I felt the same loneliness there too. The same big lock was hanging on the door, and I wondered if it was going to break. I started imagining I was a superman with supernatural powers, that laser rays would suddenly emanate from my eyes to unlock it , but I was no superman, nor do I possess supernatural skills to throw open all the barriers to my wellbeing and happiness.

Once again, I went up and lay on the cot, but immediately I felt strange warmth on my cheeks, reflecting my sad and devastated state. I kept waiting and waiting, but she didn't come nor did I get any news about her. So I again returned to those beautiful memories from my past.

Almost three weeks had passed. All of us had given up. In fact, most of us had forgotten about it. I knew that nothing would happen. I was only left with the option of ignoring her like an angel in a dream. It was as though I started the next day afresh with new ideas to forget about the past.

That night, I was turning the pages again, of 'The Fountainhead', lying on my bed, but this time more swiftly with a determination to finish it quickly. I was so fascinated by its principle and the concept of capitalism that it started getting into my psyche. While I was busy with thoughts of capitalism and about its characters, Kamal rattled me, "Where have you got lost? Lost in thoughts about her again?"

Kamal resembles a thin stick and you can see his collarbones even under his shirt, which is why we call him *Sukadbumbil*. But he was the eldest, a caring and fatherly figure without whose acceptance no resolutions could be passed. He assumed this role after one of our friends, Sarban, whom we fondly called *Chacha* because of his advice and many solutions, went back to his hometown. Since I really liked Kamal, I shared the room with him.

"No!!! I forgot whether she was ever there in my life."

"So you've lost all hope."

"If she was ever there," I stressed on the words again. To avoid further discussion about her, I buried my head in my book again.

"Okay. I didn't know that you are so weak and you will give up so early, but then I don't understand how you succeeded in your accounting exams."

"Accountancy was a question of my career."

"And she is the question of your life."

"I don't understand, Kamal, why do you want to keep this dead matter alive? What the hell do you want me to do? I cannot act like a Romeo *yaar*," I said in an irritated and slightly loud voice.

"You are already? Otherwise, why do you feel irritated with just her name?"

"Because she doesn't exist…" Before I could finish my sentence, Rathi Sahib entered our room.

He questioned, "Hey!!! What's the cause of this heated argument?"

I could not remember Rathi Sahib's original name as we all used to call him by this name because he was working with a stockbroker firm with a similar name. He was so punctual that after 9 o'clock, you would never find him anywhere other than on his bed, but somehow that day he was awake. He tried to calm things down between Kamal and me. "OK, let me try one last time for you. Perhaps my fat fingers and some luck may work for you."

When he logged into my account using the laptop, which was kept handy, a message popped up. It read, "I didn't realize that you are so desperate and mad about me that you would not hesitate to send hundreds of messages to everyone who barely resembles my name or my sister's name. Anyway, I am flattered by your style." She seemed to be a girl of few words.

Now it was Kamal's turn to create a ruckus. He duly obliged by announcing the same gleefully to the whole gang. Everyone rushed into the room as if a train was about to depart at any moment. And again, the storm started blowing, except that this time I liked it. Now it was time for a tea party. As usual, I left the room to keep myself away from the storm.

Her words kept repeating in my mind. I was not able to understand whether it was a comment or a compliment and wondered what it meant. Whatever be the case, what mattered to me the most was that she had replied. In all this, I forgot to add sugar to the tea and had to bear everyone's curses but I found it very sweet, so sweet that every part in my body could feel it. Once again, I was drowning in the image of her face.

But now the big question lay ahead of me. What next, as her message appeared to be very tricky.

5

I Heard a Whispering Voice on a Sleepless Night

Now the next question was what to do. Obviously, this again became a hot topic for debate on the floor. The message was read by almost everyone many times. A thorough analysis had started. Each and every word was interpreted like we were trying to define a new section of IPC, as though we were going to sentence a culprit. A lot of conjectures were made concerning the literal meaning as well the hidden one with the emphasis on the last sentence of the message, which read, "Anyway I am flattered by your style." Finally, there were two groups with Ashish and Abhishek insisting on proceeding aggressively while Satya and Rajiv suggested a wait and watch policy.

As I said, with that peculiar man, Rajiv, and Abhishek with his artful mind, every debate turned into a heated argument, and the rest of us stood back. Probably this was why Kamal and Rathi Sahib never took part in any discussion. They always played a neutral role. Perhaps this was done intentionally to calm both of them when they were at loggerheads. But in the end, Kamal didn't forget to make his fire-cracking remarks, which were like icing on the cake.

So how could this topic have been spared their arguments without causing them to be at loggerheads? This time I intervened. I stopped both of them, reminding them that it was my personal issue and they need not fight about it. I would see what needed to be done. I knew it would be a shock for them. Between all of us, there was no such thing as a personal matter. Everybody knew everything about everyone. After all, we were like kith and kin, and we called our group '*Chaddi-Baniyan Dost*'. We were so close that the only thing we did not share was our underwear.

The matter was laid to rest, and everybody settled into their beds. Lights were switched off and very soon all were lost in their dreams, except me. I didn't know why the goddess of sleep didn't want to do any favours tome. I became increasingly restless and continuously changed sides on the bed. My mind was full of thoughts about her and her message.

Suddenly, I heard a whimpering noise. I was bewildered. I thought it was probably from outside, but when it continued, I listened carefully. I was able to hear it clearly from the other corner of the bed.

I was surprised to hear Kamal's whispering voice. Usually, I never poke my nose into anybody's business, but I didn't know why, that day, my mind turned naughty. I gave him a shock by discovering him. I saw a very different side to Kamal - a senior citizen who had become a cool romantic guy. Mobile in his hand and headphone in his ears, he was busy talking to somebody.

He immediately disconnected the phone. He blushed with anger. He made me swear not to discuss the incident as he was going to reveal it in a day or two when everything was settled. I don't know why I trusted him. Otherwise, letting such chances go without any storm was a distant possibility. Probably I believed him because I was going through the same thing. Now I understood why he was forcing me again and again not to give up hope.

We both went back to bed. This time he asked me, "Shants, what do you think, do you really love her?"

"What type of question is this, Kamal? Of course, I do," I replied.

"What do you think you know about her? It was just a wedding party. Do you believe that you can spend the whole of your life with her after just one meeting? Don't you think it's just an infatuation?" Kamal challenged.

I sat back on the bed and replied, "Look, Kamal, I don't know whether it's just an attraction or real love. True, I don't know too much about her nature or her family background, but I am sure of one thing - her purity of thoughts and her heart, which are crystal clear. I am damn sure about her lovely innocent smile which can keep me happy for my entire life if she stays with me. Maybe I don't know if she is already committed to somebody, but I am sure of one thing, if I ever get a chance to hold her hand, I will hold it for the rest of my life. In fact, I am fully committed to her now. If love at first sight ever exists in this world, then Kamal, trust me, this is the state I am in. I love her so madly, so deeply that even if I don't meet her again, I will pray to God to give her all the happiness in this world. My love is selfless, and my feelings are pure, trust me."

"I don't need to trust you, Shants, but you need to trust yourself. If you are so certain of your love, then why are you in a state of dilemma? Just do it. Whether you get her or not doesn't matter at this stage. Am I right?"

"Hmmm." I just nodded my head, staring at the empty sky outside the window. Immediately I made up my mind. I switched on the laptop and sent her a message.

"Thanks for replying! I accept that I was completely bowled over by you when I first saw you, and I wanted to reach you by any means. Since I didn't know anything about your whereabouts, I just thought to try my luck in the virtual world, and so I sent messages to every possible name that seemed similar to yours or your sister's. But trust me it's not just attraction or lust, I really do love you, so deeply, so madly that if ever I get an opportunity to hold your hand, I will not let you down. Just give me a chance to chat with you. I will wait for your reply."

This time I did not need to wait any longer. The very next day, I got a reply that was another single line and a very ambiguous one. It didn't give even a hint of any feeling but just a message that I was not clear about. It raised many doubts in my mind. It read:

"I am just not a chat freak girl in a virtual world. Would you mind giving me a call on my telephone number?" She included her home landline number but didn't give any further details about her availability.

6

SHANTS: You Became a Fool

How would you react if you meet a girl at a marriage function, become acquainted with her through your cousin, and because you like her, later on, you start to pursue her, and she compliments you on your ways? She shared her landline number and wants you to call her on that number rather than communicating through the safer distance of the virtual world, reflecting our hi-tech generation where even a new-born baby is expected to play with a mobile or a tab.

Confusing, right?

Even I chuckled then. I thought either she or somebody else was playing tricks on me, but I was not sure about it. My heart was not ready to question or doubt her. Apart from her, only one of the six of my best friends could be the culprit, all of whom I lived with like a family. There was another reason for my suspicion, which was that except for them, nobody else knew about this and what had been done to find her.

But who the hell could it be? I wanted to find out. My mind started looking for the culprit. Rathi Sahib and Kamal were beyond doubt and were out of the question, and so I was left with four options. Satya was a genuine guy in all such matters of the heart as he was the most romantic and emotional one among us. Although he was not the focus of my suspicions, still the possibility remained as before this he had been an easy target for us, and now he could be playing this game, just for fun.

Ashish was the youngest. This was least likely from him as he always seemed too busy with his affairs, but he couldn't be ruled out because he could be easily influenced. He may not do it by choice but could do so by force. Then I was left with the options of Rajiv and Abhishek, but as Rajiv seemed very serious on this topic, I was left with no choice except for Abhishek as he had the most devious mind amongst us; he was an expert in playing such games.

Maybe all had a hand in it as had already been the case when another such incident had occurred. Satya's elder brother had once visited us for a few days, and they had used him to play a trick. Abhishek was the mastermind behind it. He got a new number and asked *bhaiya* to give me fake calls by changing his voice to sound like a girl. It was really very hard to differentiate *bhaiya's* sound from a girl on the phone since he was very soft spoken.

As I had just moved to their flat, I didn't suspect anybody either. They continued to play this game for a few days. One beautiful evening when I was busy reading my novel, I got a call from a girl calling herself my girlfriend whom I had taken for a ride, saying that she was going to commit suicide and leave behind a note naming me as responsible for her death.

I was utterly shocked and terrified to hear that I had a girlfriend that I had duped when I had never had a girlfriend until then, but she continued to issue these threats continuously for two days. I made every effort to convince her that I was not the guy she was thinking of, but all my efforts were in vain. She was not ready to listen. On the third day, being irritated, I said to her, "Please do whatever you want, including suicide if you want to, but just stop calling me."

For the next few days, I didn't get any calls. I forgot about her. Then one day, I didn't go to the office as I was not feeling well. Nobody was at home at that time except for me. I suddenly remembered that girl and got really worried and stressed that she had actually committed suicide. I called her back on that number, but nobody answered the phone. I kept on trying and trying but in vain. I did notice one thing, whenever I called that number, surprisingly I heard a simultaneous ringing in the adjacent room. I went in and checked, and to my horror,I saw the mobile screen, which gave me the shock of my life.

It read, "Shants calling." I then understood the whole picture. That night I raged at everybody, using the choicest of insults.

But this time, I was in no mood to tolerate such jokes. I might have killed someone if I found any of them were playing tricks on me but was lost as to how to catch the culprit behind all of this. I immediately googled the telephone number. I checked the code to see if it really belonged to Jaipur and found that it definitely did. So it was apparent that none of my friends was playing a game with me. But then I was flummoxed and started genuinely doubting her.

Was she playing a game with me or did she really want to talk to me? My mind was not able to accept that a girl would immediately share her number with a stranger whom she had met only once and that too her landline number instead of her mobile. My dilemma had started and in such a state, how can you live in peace?

I was sitting at my office desk lost in my world. I ignored that Bharat *bhai,* who sat two cubicles away from my workplace, had called me up twice. Now he was sitting at my desk. Bharat *bhai* was senior to me at work, and I had a very professional relationship with him until I realized the fact that he was not just an old man, but a very affectionate person as well. This was why people start calling him *bhai* as soon as they met him. Even my boss did so. Over time, he turned out to be an excellent friend and an elder brother to me so that I shared almost everything with him until now.

"Shants! What happened? Some problem? I called you twice, but you didn't pick up. Want a tea break?"

"Yeah! I really need one badly." A sleepless night had already filled me with tiredness and a kind of boredom such that I could not concentrate on anything. I called up Rajesh, my subordinate, on whom I relied entirely for my daily work. I gave him the necessary instructions and left for tea.

To lift the burden of my thoughts, I told Bharat *bhai* the complete story while sipping my tea. It was 3o' clock in the afternoon. At last, he said, "Don't leave any matter open-ended. It needs to be addressed at once to keep your mind at peace." He immediately took out his mobile from his pocket and called that mysterious number in a moment.

Ring…Ring…Ring… It rang until the line got disconnected. Nobody answered the call.

"Why don't you try in the evening? Probably no one is at home right now. She must have gone to college. We will call again in the evening," he said in a consoling tone. I just nodded my head in reply.

This time I dared calling her again in the evening. I heard a male voice at the other end. It was probably her father or brother so I immediately disconnected. Later, I tried calling her many times but every time the phone was either not answered or I heard a man's voice on the line, upon hearing which I cut short the call without uttering a word.

I didn't reach her any time, and neither did I dare speak to that male voice. The sound of "Hello?" itself was so terrible that it sent shockwaves through my body. Finally, I decided to leave a message online. It read, "I tried calling you many times. At almost every possible time when I could imagine that you might be available at home. Can you please give me a call back on my mobile? I hope you are not making a fool out of me."

I did not need to wait for long this time. The very next day I got a reply, which was just a smiley.

"☺"

Nothing more and nothing less. It was just a mark which made me irritated so that, for the first time, I cursed myself terribly. I asked the same question again and again, "How can you, Shants? You are not a Devdas or something…you always used to keep this sort of love thing at arm's length."

I thought that she was making a fool of me.

7

When Everything Boomeranged, I Was Shaken

My whole body was shaking in anger and embarrassment. "This is not the way to respond. She could have simply told me not to chase her. Why did she play the fool with me? First, she raised my hopes and then a stupid smiley? This is not how to behave. Oh God, for the first time I believed in you, and then you did this to me. Not fair at all."

My reaction was nothing but the human tendency to keep blaming God for every failure in life. But for every good event, we believe that it is due to our own efforts. I didn't believe that God had so much time to interfere in my life. Anyway, whatever God had to say on this, the result was that I was disappointed. My heart was broken into a thousand pieces.

Whenever I felt depressed, I don't know why but I always walked to Juhu Chaupati, which was just a few miles away from our home. That day too I went there and stayed a little longer than usual. There, alone, I came to appreciate the raw truth of that beautiful place.

Perhaps it was the smog that was created by the nearby beach, from the evaporation of water. The setting sun on the distant horizon attracted me most about the place. The sky continuously changed colour from light blue to orange, then finally to a dark red. When the sun was almost lost to the waves of the sea, the sky turned into pale yellow, as if paying homage to the sun that would die shortly with all its brightness left within it. Finally, the sky turned black, decorated with small little stars and the moonlight. It appeared like the graveyard of the sun was made beautiful by tiny flowers and a garland.

Below, people were busy with their affairs, completely unaware of what was happening in the outside world, dumping all their garbage on the beach that was lost for a while in the high tide, a tide that seemed to be hungry with a desire to swallow the beach entirely.

The waves kept increasing, curious to touch the various lines drawn by the children, as though they were competing with them. At that moment, nothing seemed so bad. Everything appeared excited and enthusiastic.

This fantastical place filled my mind with a sense of those tidal waves, making my heart feel alive but who knew what lay ahead. I was mesmerized at the sight of this *Mayavi Nagri.*

After dusk, everyone seemed tired. Slowly and steadily, the place started to empty. People began packing and leaving. This place that had been so full of such energy and enthusiasm became desolate and lonely.

At last, the waves also got tired and started to turn back. Earlier they had shown an appetite to swallow everything like a mischievous child but now started to retire to the depths of the sea. That was when the sea performed its duty as a mother.

It ensured that whatever rubbish was dumped into the waves instead of dustbins remained on the seashore. Everything that was mishandled had to boomerang, and it boomeranged here too. Nothing goes into it that is left behind, which appears as the dirtiest kind of sins that human beings committed during the day. Truly, it was not the kind of loneliness that boomeranged but instead the solitude when you realize your karma, making you feel naked, and everything is seen as a raw truth. Finally, the place was rank with a disgusting, stinking atmosphere.

Under the dark sky, you will see nothing. You will hear nothing but the loudness of the waves within the deep sea, as if mocking each human being, screaming, "You tried to dump me. No. It's not you but me that dumped you, with all of your disgust in your rightful place where you deserve it the most."

The most beautiful place turned into a vast dustbin. Whatever energy was generated, whatever enthusiasm was created, whatever zeal was appreciated all were lost to it and that day, I felt the same way; Disgusted and tortured.

That day, while lying on the cot under the blank sky in that cold night, I was feeling the same way:

Disgusted and tortured.

Yes, disgusted I was by the sins that I had committed in the past. Yes, tortured by the one whom I loved the most.

As if whatever wrong I had done was coming back to haunt me like the waste that was left on the seashore.

I always wondered how family violence can occur between two persons who live under the same roof and love each other so much that they will do anything for each other. But now I understood how it happens. Misunderstandings are the key, but that it could happen to me, I still couldn't believe it.

How could I? What an asshole I was. I tried to raise my hand against the one who was my life, my love, my beloved darling- my wife.

My darling wife didn't say anything. She just burst into tears and locked herself in the bedroom. The next day, she woke up silently. She completed all her daily chores meticulously but her face had lost the charm it always tended to wear. Her eyes swelled, but somehow the flood of tears had stopped, displaying her state of mind; which was hurt very badly just because of some stupid insanity of mine.

During that whole morning, our eyes never met, we didn't talk to each other at all. I meant to say sorry to her, but something stopped me. Probably because I was full of guilt or shame or some sort of chauvinistic feeling. What exactly it was, I don't know. Finally, she left like she always did and went to the office but this time in a different manner. This time she disappeared without a smile, which she tended to give me in the ordinary course of the day. Without a peck on my cheek, that she always used to plant when stealing a moment away from everyone's gaze. Without asking me to park her bike outside the home and put all her stuff into it, and lastly, without any instructions not to forget my lunchbox that she normally gave me, putting it on the dining table along with breakfast.

But wait a minute here!

My lunchbox was still lying on the dining table along with breakfast as it always did. See how lovely my wife was? I just saw her leaving silently and regretfully. What I had done to her was entirely unforgivable.

The whole day I really wanted to call her but couldn't. I did not dare to. When I reached home and found the house locked, I waited for her on this strange cot, which I had never used before. If not her, then at least waiting for her call to come but she never came nor did she call. Finally, I slipped my mobile into my pocket. All of a sudden, I felt a vibration in my pocket like the day when I was dragging my feet on the seashore, when it became utterly unbearable to sit over there.

Recalling that midnight when I was on the shore, after feeling the vibration, my hand reached into my pocket. I took out my mobile. When I saw the name on the screen, my eyes opened wide, my eyebrows squeezed together and my forehead strained. How could she call me at the eleventh hour? She had never done so before, so why today? What had happened? My mind filled with so many riddles that could not be resolved until I answered the call.

8

That Shocking
but Pleasant Call

Without any further delay, I picked up the phone and managed to say, "Hello!"

I didn't hear any words from the other side. It's not like the other person was dumbfounded by my greeting. In a passing moment, with a sigh, I realized what was going on at the other end. Since childhood, I was used to guessing things. I didn't say anything for a moment. Now I could hear sobbing on the other side.

"What happened?" My tongue made an effort to move slowly.

Now more sobbing but before long, it was suddenly broken as an effort was made to find the consolation, which was expected from me. But instead, I said, "Why do you want to hide it from me? Just let it out."

Finally, the voice completely broke, and I didn't attempt to console it. I waited until she stopped crying.

Finally, I said, "Now if you've finished crying and your drama is over, may I ask you what the heck is the matter?"

"You see, I always told you that you will never understand me. What makes you think that girls always cry and want drama? Go to hell and never talk to me again." The line was disconnected.

"Holy shit! Do girls always behave in such a mysterious way? They can't understand simple humour," I mumbled. I called her back. After a moment's pause, she picked up, but this time I could still hear her sobbing. When it became unbearable for me, I urged her to stop and smile a little. To do that, I made her realise that her mourning would do nothing good to me but only increase my distress and I was already in such an agony that I couldn't bear any more.

"Please tell me what happened? I was just joking, *yaar* but let me tell you that if you don't stop it, I will also cry with you, and I don't think you want to see me crying on this filthy night at the seashore. After seeing me in this state, these so-called constables of Mumbai might jail me for attempting suicide."

She chuckled, "Is that possible?"

"Of course! Very much. Anything is possible nowadays."

"Aah! Imagine you are in jail and I will not come to rescue you as I did last time. It will be great fun seeing you in the headlines this time."

"I know you want this to happen to me. What weird friends have I got?" I snapped.

"Well, last time it was not my fault at all. That was because of that stupid constable, my foot slipped on that ITO Bridge. I just managed to escape from falling into the Yamuna River."

"Don't tell me what happened and thank that constable who saved your life. You are a big coward, and I know it well."

"I am not a coward."

"Yes, you are. But tell me one thing, what the heck are you doing at this late hour on the seashore. Are you out of mind and do you need therapy again?"

"You bitch, you always think along the wrong lines. Now tell me, why did you call me so late and why were you crying?" I said, frustrated.

But hearing this, she burst out laughing. "Am I really?" Then she became serious. "Nothing much. I am just pissed off by this *sasu ma* of mine. She is such a creep who doesn't allow a single moment to pass without torturing me." Before she could speak more, I intervened, "Look! Now that's your home, and you love your hubby, so you need to keep your hubby happy, right!"

She mumbled, "Hmmm."

"So let's just let this difficult moment pass and try to love everyone. I know some people are difficult to win over. I don't know how but I know you will. After all, you are such a lovely and charming friend of mine who always made this world smile. One day you will win the heart of everyone."

"Will you please stop buttering me up and let me know exactly what are you doing at the seashore so late at night? I know you very well; there must be something you are hiding from me."

I told her everything in detail. She listened to my story earnestly and finally said, "Interesting. I know you will get her. Mark my words."

"I don't think so," I smiled wryly.

"Shants…"

Indeed, Tanvi was the person who had called me that night. She was one of my greatest childhood friends and my cousin too. Whatever I am today is all because of her. She kept me motivated every time I failed. She always pushed me to pursue my dreams. If she were not there, I would not have become a Chartered Accountant. I had failed my final exams for the third time. I was disappointed and lost in my thoughts, remembering my father's last warning to accept a decent job offered by Lloyds Steel in Wardha, on the recommendation of one of my uncles. I was sitting on the edge of the ITO Bridge, considering giving up the idea of becoming an accountant and accepting the offer instead. But suddenly out of nowhere, a constable appeared. He thought I was trying to commit suicide. He shouted from behind me. I was bewildered. Before I could get down from the edge, my leg slipped, but somehow the constable managed to catch hold of me, and I was saved.

He insisted on talking to my parents before letting me go so I called Tanvi, who ably pretended to be my mother and convinced him to release me without making any more fuss.

Following her marriage, she was staying with her in-laws in Merut while her husband stayed in Chandigarh. At times, she faced that similar music of *saas-bahu*, which every Indian woman is poised to experience, and instead of disturbing her caring husband, she shared her woes with me. I just listened as her best friend, which made her feel better. What else I could do? If she was happier after sharing it with me, I always loved to do the same for her. After all, she was still my best friend though now she called whenever she felt like it, which was only once in a blue moon as we both were busy in our day to day lives.

"I told you that one day you will be in love, very true and divine love and here you are. I will pray for you. You will definitely get her. I would bet on it," she said confidently.

"No betting please, just pray for me. Take care of yourself."

She hung up. I set out for home feeling lighter now. You always feel lighter when you know there is someone in this lonely world who will at least pray for your happiness. Don't you?

9

Satya- the Numerologist/Palmist

That night Tanvi had called me to soothe me but on this sad night when I was lying on the cot, who was calling me?

"Oh dear, is that you? Please tell me that you really want to talk to me again." My heart cried. "Please come back."

It took all my energy to get my mobile out. When I saw the name flashing on the screen, I felt a bit relieved in the hope that now I would get some news about my dear wife. The screen flashed the name - Megha - my dearest sister-in-law - the most charming character that I have ever met in this world with her prominent dimpled smile.

As soon as I answered the phone and before I could utter a single word, she just blurted out, "*Jiju!* How can you do that to my sister? How dare you bring tears to her eyes? I know her, she is not going to tell me the complete fucking story, so it's better you tell me. What the hell is going on?"

"No dear, it's nothing. She is just overreacting to the situation. It happens in every family. I think we can sort out the issues by discussing it."

Before I could complete my sentence, she said, "She is not overreacting to the situation, but it's you and by the way, what the hell is this damn Mishika doing in your life?"

That question of hers filled me with anger again, and this time I cut her short. "Megs! You better mind your language before speaking to me like that. I am listening but it doesn't mean that I will take any shit from anybody. Better you explain to your sister that she should talk to me directly rather than approaching it this way." I hung up without giving any further explanation.

Instead of getting relief, my mind was completely disturbed. Now I felt confused. I closed my eyes and lost myself in my old world of a few years back when I was on that seashore and somewhat relieved by Tanvi's call.

When I reached home, Satya was anxiously waiting for me. He kept pacing the room over and over. As soon as I entered the flat, he bombarded me, "Where the hell were you? I was trying to call you for ages but as usual, your phone was not reachable."

"Oh yeah, its battery is dead," I said, which was a constant and real problem for me. Whenever a person is desperately trying to reach me, my phone is always dead. I don't know why it happens, but it does so every time.

"Anyway, what happened? Why were you looking for me so desperately?"

"Did you happen to check your fucking account? What were you up to? Why are you doing this?" Satya almost shouted at me.

"Why? What happened? For God's sake, will you guys please stop spying on me? She ditched me. I will never forgive her for this," I said irritably.

"What did you say? She ditched you. You cowardly scoundrel, you made her life hell. First, tell me whether you have checked your account or not?" Satya said.

"Yeah, I checked. It was just a smiley that she has messaged. She ruined all my dreams with that damned smiley," I said in a disgusted voice.

"Then you need to check something more," Satya said to me while handing over the laptop. It was a message from her which read:

"You are such a coward that you made my father furious with your calls. It's better you stay away. You don't deserve to be called a man."

I was bewildered to see this message. I laughed at my situation and my mind was more confused.

"Yes, my dear friend. This is it. See what you did. Let me help you this time. Show me your palm. I will tell you when to call her," Satya said. He was a firm believer in numerology and palmistry. He practiced it religiously. Many times he had told me to be guided by it, but I tended to ignore him because for me they are just tools to make fools of people and print money doing so.

"I am not going to call her. If she feels that way, then she can call me. If she has an attitude then I too have an attitude. It is nothing to do with your fake mysticism. And I am in no mood to listen to that."

"My dear friend, it's not mysticism but pure science. A science -based on precise mathematical calculations and the analyses of planetary alignment at the time people are born. Every person is ruled by planets. He or she shows certain characteristics because of the planet they are ruled by. Hence by analysing them, we can discover the strength and power of planets using one's palm and try to find out how successful they can be in their endeavours."

"So it means you can decide the future and luck of people through your fake science. If you can, then why the hell can't you guys stop these natural calamities?"

"My dear friend, weather forecasting depends on different tools, but this science is based on practical knowledge and analysis of the location of the planets. If you know your exact date of birth and time, then you can forecast your luck too. Luck is just a ratio of output versus input. In good times, one gets a higher proportion and in bad times the ratio decreases. So this analysis is mainly a tool, which helps one in maximizing good times and minimizing the risk at bad times. Anyway, whether you believe in it or not, it doesn't matter here. What harm will it do if you try it once? Who knows if luck may work for you this time?"

I was in no mood to argue with Satya on this topic, so I just let it pass. I cooperated with him in whatever he wanted me to do. He did some odd calculations and suggested that I call her between 8 and 9 o'clock in the morning.

"For God's sake, no, please. This science of yours, it's going to be a total flop. That is when her father and brother are both at home. Also, by that time she will have already left for college."

"See, you have already lost hope, so why don't you try it just once?" Satya insisted, adding, "I will bet on this. If I lose, I will give you a party but otherwise you will take us out."

Though in the depth of my heart I was thoroughly convinced that this was not going to work, in any case, I was in a win-win situation. This was the only type of bet I would take. So I accepted the gamble. I decided to go with Satya's suggestion and take one last chance.

The challenge given was announced on the floor by Satya, and everybody waited for the fateful morning.

The next morning, the alarm clock hanging on the wall rang at 8 o' clock. Everybody came close to me to share the next few but crucial seconds. Once again, I called her on her landline. After a very long time, somebody picked up. And when I heard the voice saying, "Hello" my whole body started shaking. My mind went numb. My tongue refused to respond. I broke into a sweat, and my legs struggled to remain still.

Seeing my situation, everybody's jaws dropped and the colour of their faces changed. Everybody stared at Satya as though he was the worst culprit on this earth. The best punishment for such a heinous crime was that he should be hanged to death. Satya was just not able to believe what was happening.

I disconnected the phone hastily without uttering a single word. I stood up, still stunned.

Everybody was pretty sure of what had happened, and they were just waiting for me to speak but before I could react, Abhishek, the most aggressive amongst us, started ornamenting his language with the foulest language that exists on this earth. "I told you not to trust him. Now face the consequences."

Rajiv hissed, "Bastard! He was not able to handle his own love story, and poked his nose in others'. And you, Shants, why do you believe such a *fakologist?*"

"Rajiv!! Why did you drag my love story into this and please mind your words! That was not a love story at all," Satya retorted defensively.

"Ooh! Then who the hell is Preha? Don't tell me, Satya," yelled Rajiv.

"Rajiv, please, don't drag Preha into everything." Satya almost shouted now.

"Guys, please stop blaming Satya." I interrupted while letting myself fall onto the bed. "Whatever happened is over now so please stop humiliating Satya. You guys deserve a party, and you will get it. It doesn't matter from whom? Let this moment pass."

"But who did you talk to? Was that her father? Why has your face turned so pale?" Kamal questioned me, still not able to believe the turn of events, but at this question, everyone went silent. The silence was so deafening that even if a pin had dropped, you would have heard it. Silence itself is very unusual in our flat, but if there is dead silence, then it means something is exceptionally amiss. Everyone was eager to know about the incident as I could see by their faces.

Finally it was time to break the silence, and it broke in the way that it deserved.

10

Finally the
Silence Was Broken

"Friends… Satya made every effort to make me successful. It doesn't matter whether I succeed or not. As he said, it doesn't matter to try once like this as I'm in a win-win situation. So guys, let's party together."

Upon hearing this, the jaws of all those present dropped in disbelief. Everybody wanted to see this happen, but not in that way, and now I could sense that all were curious to know the story. All of them were waiting for more details. When it came to a party, we were all keen but this time even news of a party was not able to excite them. Of all of them, the most anxious was Satya. I could see that Satya made greater efforts to speak of this as if it was a question of life and death.

He exclaimed, "What? First, tell us what has happened?"

"Nothing! Are you afraid of sponsoring the party now? Guys, why worry? We will party together today at the best place like Satya said," I replied without any expression on my face.

Now I could see that even Satya had put down his weapons. He had accepted defeat. He lumbered a bit and then sank his body in the plastic chair nearby. The chair appeared to be like a bed of thorns to him.

"Guys, lets decide when and where," I cried. "What does it matter now? We always celebrated whether it's good news or bad." But nobody seemed to hear me. All of them started moving off to do their daily chores.

"Friends, is the news of a party sponsored by Satya so bad that you all are afraid of a stomach disorder? If that is the case, then don't worry, let me host the party."

"What?" Everybody challenged me as one. This time, before anybody could react, Satya came forward. He grabbed me by my shirt's collar and said, "You scoundrel! Don't play games with us. It was her, wasn't it?"

"Yes. It was her".

"Tell us the complete story, you fucking idiot, or else I will kill you today." Satya was gnashing his teeth and pushing me towards the bed. I could see everybody grinding their teeth like angry wolves.

It was her sweet voice that had melted in my ear. She'd rendered me speechless so that I felt like a statue. She had answered the call and said, "I am really very sorry. I wanted to talk to you badly but now I am rushing to college. Also, everybody is waiting for me at the breakfast table so I will call at night. ."

Before I could finish my sentence, I felt a sudden pain on my back. Before I could react, I felt pain emanating from my cheek followed by a hard hit on my bum. I lost my balance and fell on the bed. I don't remember what happened after that; I received a flurry of punches, bumps and several blows. I remember it was started by Satya, followed by a slap from Rajiv, and Abhishek from behind, hitting my bum, and finally it was all of them together.

When they got tired, they lifted me up. They started marching like I had won World War III and was returning from the field like a hero. All were crying together:

"Here is our first martyr...

Here is our first hero...

No matter what ground it was...

He won Ground Zero..."

Followed by slogans... *Zindabad... Zindabad...* Shants... *Zindabad...*

Still, the words echoed in my mind, as I lay upon the cot. Now also I remembered their excitement, enthusiasm and energy as they lifted me up. Even now, I could feel those caring thumps to my head, my back and all over my body.

Friends...

Oh, my dear friends...

Once again, I need you...

Once again, I feel for you…

Wherever you are…

Come and lift me up…

From this *Shar Saiya*…

I am not the Bheesma of Mahabharata.

Who can lie comfortably on a bed of arrows?

With a self-proclaimed wish for death.

I am not that great that I can see that entire epic, the Mahabharata, with my eyes alone.

I cannot see my love leaving like this, leaving me in limbo.

Once again, please drive the chariot as Krishna did for Arjuna.

Oh, my dear friends.

Are you listening?

I am not Bheeshma but a common man with a very uncommon pain.

Come, lift me up.

I need you. I feel you here, right now, by my side.

I don't know why my dry eyes again started flooding with tears that flowed continuously. My whole face, my entire shirt was wet from the flood like that day, when I was lifted up by my friends with their hands.

I was not the fat and paunchy guy then that I am now. I was a thin, skinny and average looking guy. They just threw me onto the bed.

It was a ground rule in our flat, not imposed by our owner but strictly enforced by Kamal, our fatherly friend that, whatever be the occasion, liquor would not enter our house. But for the first time, this rule was broken, and you can't imagine, who broke it.

When we were arguing about the venue for the party, Kamal said, "Let's just party at home. God knows when she will call and what we will be doing at that time. It may happen that this dear friend of ours misses the chance to talk to her. It may give her an opportunity to be angry with him, nevertheless she will, and we can't stop it, but I don't want to be blamed for that. I know him very well. He will not say anything, but he only wants this to happen now. Isn't that right, Shants?

I just nodded.

"But can you imagine the party without liquor." This was Rajiv who was a bit disappointed.

"Who said without liquor? You take responsibility for making all the arrangements. Also, this will be covered by our flat funds. Let us celebrate together now for our friend," Kamal instructed.

"But what about your rule?" Satya quizzed.

"Sometimes rules have to be broken for friends," Kamal said, while wrapping his arm around my neck.

"Ouch!" I cried out loudly.

"What happened?" all of them asked me.

"Kamnio itna jor jor se mara hai tumne, ki mera jarra jarra dard se karah raha hai." (Bastards you have beaten me so badly that every part of my body is in pain.)

"Oye no more sadi hui shayri please…vaise abhi tak mere hath mai kujli ho rahee hai," (Don't give us damn excuses by your useless *shayari*. I still feel that I should thrash you more) Abhishek shouted. With this, he started running behind me. We were running like Tom and Jerry, from one room to another, jumping from one bed to the next, from the stairs to the roof until finally, I locked myself in aroom to save myself from getting another thrashing.

"Nautanki sala… he deserves this." I could hear their loud laughter.

7.30 PM

We all left the office early. All the arrangements had been made by Rajiv and Abhishek. Rum, beer, *paneer tikka*, and peanut *masala* for snacks and the four-course dinner that was already ordered.

We all were at home by then except for Ashish.

Rajiv called him. "Hey where are you? Have you done the job which I gave you?"

"Yes bro… just reaching in another ten minutes. I have done everything," Ashish replied.

When Ashish came in, he took out something from his bag wrapped like a gift, but before anybody could get a look at it, Rajiv snatched it away and kept it safe.

I was asked if I had received any call. I said, "No, not yet. She told me that she would call at night so probably at 9.30 or so."

8.00 PM

"Yeah, it's already eight. Let's start the party now." Before the party could start Ashish appeared with a *puja thali*, fully decorated and arranged. Then he put it on the centre table.

Rajiv said, "Before the start of every good thing, we call for our deity *(Devta)*. You know here we have a very special *Devta*. Do you know what it is? Any wild guesses?"

Everybody seemed to be puzzled. What could it be? We had never had any such tradition before a party so now, what was this? Was it something related to what Ashish had brought?

Rathi Sahib and Abhishek seemed a little worried and questioned, "After all, what is he up to?" Finally, Abhishek said, "Rajiv, if it really is something related to God, then I think we should stop doing that. After all, it's our religion. We should respect it and should not play games with it."

For the first time, we saw Abhishek turn stern.

"Don't worry. We will not hurt anybody's feelings. You just keep guessing," Ashish replied.

Once again, we all were in a quandary and banging our heads together.

11

And the Party Goes On...

Before we could make any wild guesses, it was Rajiv who threw another bit of philosophy at Abhishek.

"Mr Abhishek! What if I tell you that this is the idol of the God you pray to? We are going to worship it by liquor, does it matter to you? God is everywhere and in every particle, and it's just an idol. Isn't it?

"Rajiv that's enough. Don't dare to speak anything about my religion. Don't forget that you also belong to the same community. I know you are an atheist, but still, I am not going to tolerate it."

"Oh!! See the fanatics. In the name of religion, they can bleed the blood of innocents. They can behead people, loot and rape the girls and women and can act in whatever cruel way they want and still they demand that we preach such religion. Fuck your religion and goddamn it, fuck you." Rajiv had started almost panting, uttering these powerful words. For the first time, we were seeing him so aggressive, but it was not just Rajiv who was boiling.

We could see Abhishek's face too was changing colour at Rajiv's words.

He was wild. He started his part of the argument so loudly that the whole building could hear it very clearly. "You scoundrel! Don't even dare to speak a single word against my religion; otherwise, I don't know what will happen next. To hell with you, I know what sort of cruelty and atrocities you are referring to. Listen to me with utmost care; what happened in the Gujarat riots was 500% correct and I stand by it. It was just a reaction to what those bastards did. They very well deserved it. They understood that we Hindus have worn bangles in our hand that we don't know how to cut. A lesson needed to be taught to them, and this is exactly what we have done. If it is in my hands, I will behead all of these traitors and make our country free from these evils. Bastards! *Jis thali mai khate hai usi mai ched karte hai.* (They always stab us in the back.)Just because of your secularism and dirty politics, this country is suffering. Our Bharat *Ma* is bleeding."

"What a stupid concept. Godhra was just the reaction of something, and there has to be some other anti-reaction to it. Tell me up to what point this mania will continue like this, this bloodbath will continue and people have to suffer. Up to what point will our children have to be orphaned. Tell me up to what point humanity has to be crushed and destroyed. Haven't we suffered a lot? Now stop it, just for the sake of your God only. You know what, it's not these people who are destroying the country but people like you, who in the name of fanaticism and religion are destroying this country."

"Then why the hell don't you see another side of it. Didn't we suffer? Every time, after every blast, why these *kattus'* name occurred? What do you think, our children are not children but dogs, our sisters and mothers are not mothers and sisters but their toys who can tolerate their atrocities? Our …"

"STOP IT RIGHT NOW… BOTH OF YOU… JUST STOP."

They both were almost hissing. Before they wrestled with each other, before we saw any further rounds of mania, before our neighbours came and before the mood of the party got ruined, though none of us seemed to be excited about it now, Kamal asserted his authority. He used his veto power to end any more discussion.

"Now both of you, end this right now right away else I am gonna throw both of you out of this house. Ashish! stop all this nonsense. Let that thing remain wrapped for now."

"But *bhaiya*… there is nothing in it which will disturb anybody over here." He quickly unwrapped the package. When we all saw it, our eyes widened in astonishment.

It was a beautifully designed mobile stand made of wood. Ashish continued, "We all know about Shants *bhai*, how careless he is about his mobile and we all know that he never picks it up in one ring. We all know how important this mobile *devta* is today. If he missed it again, we don't know how *bhabhi* will react, so just to ensure that nothing goes wrong, we planned for it."

Satya made us laugh with his hilarious proverb, "*Lai kya baat thi or kya ho gaya…khoda pahad nikli chuhiya.*"

(What we are trying to do over here is making a mountain out of a molehill.)

"It is he who started it. We just asked what was in it," Abhishek murmured.

"It is me!! It is me who started it. It's you who got excited before we could explain anything," Rajiv hissed.

"Okay, leave it both of you and join hands. Let's party hard now," Kamal said.

8.30 PM

The party started as planned. 'Mobile *devta*' was placed in between in the stand, which was the culprit for the entire act we had witnessed just now. It was worshipped religiously, and both Abhishek and Rajiv had prayed to it very loudly. After that, we started drinking. Rounds of pegs and shots, rounds of light discussion, rounds of hilarious non-vegetarian jokes, and rounds of all sorts of vulgarity. What do you expect from a bachelor party? But the mobile *devta* didn't budge. Every ten minutes, we would turn silent. One of us would get up and check the mobile, which was placed on the table in the centre of the hall.

11.30 PM

While we were enjoying, neither did the mobile *devta* budge nor did we lose hope. We continued to have rounds of shots. Finally, our dinner too was over. Everybody lay down wherever he was, and whatever the situation he was in, except for me.

My eyes were continuously staring at the table in the centre. Finally, I too became tired; I walked out of the flat.

I stood near the open balcony, which was situated on the landing.

I stood with the support of the railing, allowing all my weight to fall on my hands, leaning forward, head down, heartbroken, disappointed and distressed and just waiting. The whole night was covered by dead silence.

You know what, waiting for something is the most significant punishment on this earth. If somebody does a crime, just let him wait for his fate. Indeed, one day he will be broken mentally and physically. He will cry out loudly - *punish me*, he will pray for his life to be saved from the suffocation of waiting but don't allow him to come out. One day, he will die out of the torture of waiting. Imagine if such a dangerous punishment is given to an innocent man?

Whether I am innocent or a culprit, this will be decided by time, these incidents must show it, and I leave it to you to determine my fate.

But anyway, as of now, when I was lying on the cot on that deadly cold night, I was suffering from a similar fate. It's like time was not moving at all. Suddenly I felt something touched my shoulder. It was a very gentle touch. I didn't turn in astonishment but closed my eyes and took a deep breath.

I murmured, "Mishh, I know it's you, right! I know it's your touch. I know you will never leave me alone. Never ever, especially in these difficult times. You promised you will always remain with me. Always forever. Now speak up, Mishh. Why are you not speaking anything? Can't you see that I am sobbing? Do you want me to be seen as the weakest person on this earth? Why are you not passing your sarcastic comments? Can't you see that I am waiting?" But no answer came. Finally, I became restless and irritated as I used to get in office when she didn't reply to me.

I turned back. I could see her smiling face in front of me. "Heroine!! Have you turned deaf and dumb?"

"Shants!! Please calm down and listen to me. I didn't go anywhere. I am with you as I said, always and forever. Why can't you see me? We have seen so many bad phases in life, and you know very well that everything will pass eventually. Trust me, this too shall pass. Nothing is immortal on this earth, neither pain nor happiness. So please don't overreact. Now I have to go. Bye, and take care." She looked at her watch and suddenly disappeared like a ghost.

"Mishh… Mishh… are you there? Where have you gone? Was I dreaming of her or was she really with me?" I heard something downstairs. I left the idea of a ghost for the time being and concentrated on listening to what was happening below.

The telephone in the room was ringing. I ran downstairs. All of a sudden, I didn't know from where, I found the strength within me. But the door was firmly locked. I quickly looked for options to unlock it. The phone was still ringing. I ran here and there, up and down, looking for something which could break open the lock. Then I found a big sharp stone. I started banging it on the bolt.

I banged a few times. The lock seemed to be stubborn. It didn't want to lose its latch so quickly, but this time, I was more determined. I made a few more quick bangs and finally, it accepted defeat, and the latch loosened. How could a little lock stop a determined person? I broke into the house, but just then, the telephone stopped ringing. Once again, I had lost. What was I supposed to do? Should I call her or should I wait for a few moments? The dilemma was the same as the day of the party when I was supposed to receive her call for the first time.

12.00 AM

I was standing in the balcony, staring at the pale sky. I was thinking of the heated argument between Abhishek and Rajiv. This is the tragedy of our country - how people go crazy in the name of religion. How many *babas* have come and gone, claimed themselves to be the God, looted the public not only of wealth but also of health and the power to discern right and wrong with their myths. Probably it's not the devotion within us, but the fear which they have created in the name of God and religion, that we are supporting them blindly.

Suddenly, I felt that my mobile *devta* was ringing.

I ran downstairs but to my surprise, I found that the door was locked. Then I realized what could have gone wrong. We had a central locking system in our door, and because of the wind, it must have closed. This was a prevalent problem in Mumbai.

"Holy shit," I shouted and tried to ring the doorbell but alas, even that was not working. I remembered that in the morning Kamal had given instructions to Babloo to call for the electrician and get it repaired but as usual, Babloo wouldn't act until he was reminded multiple times.

I banged the door, but nobody heard. Alcohol was playing its game. It had already captured their minds and bodies. Rathi Sahib was the only hope because he'd never had liquor in his life, but he must have been sleeping in his bedroom behind another door so it was unlikely that he would hear me. Also, he slept very deeply.

"What to do? What to do?" My mind was working very fast. I was considering all the options very quickly. I tried again and banged the door a little louder, shouting several times. Nothing happened. If I had slammed it loudly, there was a risk that instead of these drunkards, our neighbours would come out.

I thought of another option, and that option was the intercom. Maybe that could awake these Kumbhakarnas. I ran downstairs and ran towards the security room where I could find the intercom easily. I tried from the intercom. No answer. I tried twice then thrice, but nothing worked. The security guy sensed my despair. He suggested I call one of them on their mobiles. I did know that Rathi Sahib always kept his mobile near him because of the alarm, so that was my only hope. But before I could try out this option, another tragedy struck. Who remembers the mobile number of anyone when your mobiles do the work for you? I cursed myself and looked for another option.

Then I remembered that another group of friends lived in the building next to ours in the same complex. Hopefully, they would not have slept by now. If not, I could take a risk and awaken them. I ran towards their flat. I was right; they were about to go to sleep, but my luck worked. Ashutosh opened the door. He was a bit surprised to see me there, but there was no time to explain.

Without wasting any further seconds, I quickly asked him to call Rathi Sahib on his mobile. Thankfully, he had his number. He called Rathi Sahib and handed over the phone to me. I heard Rathi Sahib's sleepy voice 'hello!' As soon as I told him the story, he jumped out of bed. He checked my mobile to see if it was still ringing. I was hoping it was. At least he could pick up the phone and ask her to wait for my call.

But nothing of that sort was happening. He mentioned that there were three missed calls from an unknown mobile number. Since I was not expecting anybody else's calls, it must have been her. Before he could pity me, I asked him to open the gate and disconnected the line.

Ashutosh was confused at what was happening. Without any explanation, I thanked him and returned to my building. While returning, when I was just about to board the lift, I saw the security man running towards me. I stopped and waited for him. He handed over an envelope to me.

"Sahib… *aaj din mai ek ladki aayi thi… wo mujhey aap logo ko dene ke liye boli thi… mai bhool gaya ise aapke* drop box *mein dalna."* (Sahib today a girl had come and asked me to give it to you but I forgot to put it in your drop box).

Many questions burst into my mind. "Who was this girl? Why did she come to handover this in person? Why didn't she post it directly?" I was already playing with puzzles. I had one more problem added to the game.

Anyway, when I saw the name on the envelope, I was shocked. It was like history was being repeated again. Now and even then. Then also, when I was struggling to get into my home due to the locked door, I was handed over an envelope by the security guard, and now also, when I struggled to open the locked gate of my home on the night when I was stuck on the roof, I found an envelope lying near the door like it had been carelessly thrown by a postman.

Then too I was shocked to see it, even now I was almost about to get a heart attack. Then too it threw a cold, sad wave on all of us, now also I was nearly shattered. Then too it brought news of separation, even now it was tearing us apart, but there was a difference. It was a happy ending then but now, time was going to tell us what lay ahead.

12

The Mystery of the Envelope

12.30 AM

The letter was intended for Satya. The sender was mentioned as Preha. What we heard from Rajiv last was that she had ditched him. Satya never told us anything. According to him, they were just good friends. Nothing more, nothing less. After hearing Rajiv's part of the story, we never forced him to tell us. On that day, the last nail was hammered into the coffin of that story. It was quite long back, probably a month ago.

Preha was our colleague who had joined the office together with us. If we want to define her beauty, you can imagine it by this - that practically every guy in the office wanted to be her friend. But because of her shrewd, egoistic and arrogant nature, it was only Satya who was able to develop some sort of relationship with her. This was the only reason we had started calling him a love guru.

We always understood it as friendship, except for Rajiv. He felt that she was misusing him by acting as his girlfriend. Satya still ignored the topic. But all of a sudden, a month back she resigned and left at a point in time when she was doing very well. She didn't meet anybody, not even Satya and left even without serving a single day's notice period. Rajiv proved Satya wrong. We observed that Satya was a little dejected, but after some time, everything became normal. But whenever Rajiv mentioned her, Satya's anger knew no bounds.

Now when everything was buried deep down in the earth, this letter had arrived after a month from nowhere. Who was the girl who had delivered the letter? Was it Preha or somebody else? Was she staying in Mumbai? Why, after one month, did she want to come back into Satya's life? What made her come here? Questions and questions - thousands of questions were floating in my mind. The only way I could get an answer was to open the letter, but I decided to hand it over to Satya.

When I reached the flat, I saw that all were fast asleep or rather, thoroughly drunk and unconscious. Only Rathi Sahib was standing in front of me. He was looking at me questioningly, like asking 'now what'?

I checked my mobile. I found three missed calls from an unknown number, which seemed to be a mobile number. I was sure it was her. I wanted to call her back, but I didn't dare considering the time. Earlier she had told me that she didn't have a mobile. I was not sure whose mobile she had called from. It could be her father's or her brother's. Only God knew about it at that time.

Suddenly Rathi Sahib asked me "What's in your hand?" That reminded me of the envelope.. I said, "Oh! It is for Satya." And kicked Satya, who was lying there, on his butt.

"Hey! What are you doing? Give it to him in the morning. Why so much hurry?"

"You know what, it's from Preha. I can't wait anymore to know about this. Don't know what sort of story this guy is cooking so I can't wait. Got to know right now, right away." While talking, I kicked him once more, but he didn't respond at all.

I picked up a water bottle, which was lying nearby, and poured it on him until it was empty.

Satya woke up in haste, cursing loudly. He was so loud that everybody woke up too. All of them looked astonished at what was happening.

"Shants, what happened? Did she call you?" It was Rajiv.

"Guys! Forget about that as of now. I have bigger news than that. This friend of ours - Satya got a letter, and guess what… who has sent this letter? This is from Preha. Yes, from the same Preha who left him in the lurch one month back?"

"WHATTTT??????" everybody exclaimed together like they had been thrown into a vessel of boiling water.

1.00 AM

Satya made a failed attempt to snatch the envelope from my hand but I didn't let him. Now I was getting really impatient. Without wasting much time, I tore the envelope and pulled out the letter from it. It was a foolscap sheet with a nicely written letter in beautiful handwriting.

Abhishek shouted, "Read loudly. We all want to listen," and everybody else supported him. "Bastard kept the story away from us. This is his punishment."

Satya looked at me sheepishly with frightened eyes, but I didn't show any mercy to him. I started reading it. All his secrets were going to be revealed very soon. Rajiv seemed to be convinced that his part of the story was going to be proved right again.

Once again, I looked at Satya. He had accepted defeat. He sat by the side of the wall and waited as if he was going to be pierced. I thought of being polite and giving him the letter but the rest would have pounced on me and stopped me from handing over the letter. So I started reading it loudly…

Dear Sattu,

"Oho… *sattu… kya baat, kya baat…*" Abhishek mocked. Satya, however, didn't react.

But as I read the first line, I could not proceed with it loudly. I read the full letter in one go, and by the time I reached the last line, my eyes were filled with tears. Everyone was troubled when they saw my tears. Before I could react, Rajiv snatched it from my hand. He reacted in the same way when he read the letter.

From Rajiv to Abhishek, Abhishek to Kamal… as it moved on, we all became silent. Meanwhile, when I looked at Satya, his eyes were closed. He seemed completely lost in his thoughts.

Finally, Rajiv shook him. He forced him to come back to the present and handed over the letter to him. Once again, he closed his eyes. Then it happened, not exactly the way we had thought but slowly and gradually.

It was happening word by word, sentence by sentence. It was like slow poisoning. It seemed that every word of the letter brought forth thousands of tears for Satya. Finally, when the ocean of tears dried, his eyes were all red, puffed, tired, lost and utterly blank, as if death had already captured his soul.

Suddenly we saw the glitter in his eyes like it was the last light from a dying candle. We were fearful. He rose up silently and started walking out. I tried to block his way. He forced me to move to the side. He then quietly walked out. He took the stairs and went to the roof.

When he was gone, all our eyes met in sudden agreement, devastated with fear. We all ran towards the stairs, but before we could reach the top, we heard a deadly sound, like something had fallen down. All of us turned numb out of horror and terror.

13

That Fatal Night

1.45 AM

All of us were petrified by the sound. Suddenly our legs went faster as if we were racing for the gold medal in the Olympics. We were racing against time, against death, against love, against friendship and this was the time to show our real strength.

When we reached the top, we all were panting heavily, but to our relief, we saw Satya sitting on the boundary. Three of us looked down to understand what had really happened? Satya seemed to be unaware of us. Rajiv, Kamal and I carefully approached him, like a lion trying to reach its prey silently, so that we wouldn't make him uncomfortable.

Kamal slowly and carefully placed his hand on Satya's shoulder. He turned and got down from the boundary wall but didn't speak a single word. Meanwhile, the watchman too had arrived on the roof. He told us that a loose brick had fallen down. Satya turned and explained that when he was trying to climb up on the boundary wall, it had fallen down. Thankfully, there was no one there at that time. No casualties were reported. The watchman took stock of the situation and went downstairs after warning us. Rajiv took him aside and explained the entire situation. Basically, in lieu of a little bribe, he had to be convinced that he could cook any sort of story behind the fall of the brick except that we all were present on the roof at midnight.

Satya placed his hand on my shoulder and said to all of us, "Guys! Don't you worry that I am gonna commit suicide just because of it? I am not that weak. Haven't you read the letter where she wants me to go ahead in life and become successful? Haven't you? So how can I be so afraid to accept this hard-core reality? Just want to be all alone for some time, so if you all permit, please!"

Nobody spoke a single word. Kamal placed his hand on Satya's shoulder in consolation but didn't say anything. I believe Satya understood his words from his eyes, which meant that *we trust you*. He asked all of us to leave him alone.

But when we were on the stairs, Kamal looked at him again and sat down. He said, "Though I believe him but still want to keep an eye on him, so you guys leave, and I will take care of him."

These were the type of friends we were - always together and with each other in sorrow and happiness.

2 AM

After reaching downstairs, I glanced towards mobile *devta,* who was lying over there silently without any movement, like an idol in a temple. But feelings and the trust behind that were so strong that I believed that it was nothing less than a God for me. I was acting like his perfect devotee. And as an ideal devotee, I had to follow the path of enlightenment too. I was in a dilemma as to which was the right way to go. I shrugged all the thoughts and hid my face beneath the bed sheet presuming that sleep would capture me very soon. But it was impossible to sleep in such a situation.

I was thinking of her. I repeatedly cursed myself, "Why the hell did I go out? If I would not have gone, I would have been talking with her, Satya would have been soundly sleeping, Kamal would not have been sitting on the stairs, Rajiv would not have been assigning hourly duty for the rest of us to look after Satya and all of us would not have been struggling with sleep."

When the guilt reached its limit, I got up, slipped my mobile into my pocket, picked up the last bottle of Kingfisher strong beer, which had somehow been left by the drunkards, and went upstairs without uttering a word.

Abhishek might have seen me going out. I just heard his extreme sarcasm in a distant voice, "*Ab hame* round duty *marne ki koi jarurat nahi hai, do devdas pahuch gaye hai ek sath, Sirf kuch aur bottles ka intezam karna hoga.*" (We don't need to do round duties as two 'Devdas' are together now. We just need to arrange a few more bottles for them.) But nobody seemed to laugh at this joke, as the atmosphere was still severe and grim.

When I reached upstairs, I asked Kamal to go down and assured him that nothing would go wrong. I approached Satya. I stood next to him without uttering a single word. I took a long gulp from the bottle of beer and offered the rest of the drink to Satya.

He looked at me once, and while maintaining silence, he followed the same sequence with the bottle which I did, but the end was slightly different. After gulping it down completely, he carelessly threw the bottle behind in the air like a plane. It floated in the air for a while, did some dancing and crash-landed on the roof. It broke the silence for a while, but that noise was hardly able to draw Satya's attention. He was sitting there as still as an idol, staring at the city right in front of us.

Lonely roads, stray dogs, rarely passing cars with unusual noises and the dead silence with cold and strong winds made the whole environment appear ghostly. It was similar to when I'd waited for Aaisha's call for a long time earlier. I sat near the telephone, staring at it continuously, like waiting for hours for a man who has gone into a coma, and the doctor hopes that he may come alive at any moment.

After a long time, I wanted to go out for some fresh air; however, it was chilly outside. The walls of the room appeared like I was in jail. On my way out, I found an envelope lying near the door, thrown by somebody carelessly. I quickly opened it. When I saw the first highlighted line of the letter, I just froze. I felt like thousands of hammers were being hit on my head simultaneously.

I came in, washed my eyes with cold water and then again looked at the letter, but the result was the same. Still, I was not able to believe my eyes. Again I rubbed my eyes, splashed a lot of water into my eyes, continued the same sequence for a while and then again looked at it but it did not help. The result was the same.

It was a divorce notice from the lawyer. I couldn't dare to read it further. The letter fell from my hands. I couldn't believe that this could ever happen to me. That too for such a small incident… No… No…Please let me rectify…it was not that small as it appeared to me but still not too big either that she should take such a harsh step. I was wondering why she was not allowing me to explain even once. In this world, there is nothing which can't be explained. I knew I could explain.

I was still wondering what made her take such an extreme step. If that was the case, then what made her prepare breakfast and lunch for me? Was it because she wanted to do it for her caring husband one last time?

Caring husband… my foot…

This was the reward you got for all your caring. Yes, Shants, this was the reward for you, and probably you deserved this. But my dear, did you take our son's future into consideration before making such a bewildering decision? I couldn't think anything further. Only that one word was echoing in my mind like the way, that time, Satya's letter had echoed in my mind…DIVORCE… DIVORCE… DIVORCE…

14

The Letter

Dear Sattu,

By the time you will be reading this letter, I will not be there to see your reaction. This is the saddest part of my life. If I had powers, I would have stopped this time or requested God to stay this time for a while but alas! Neither do I have such skills nor does God approve such requests. How helpless we people are against a decision of this nature… You'll see.

I badly wanted to see your reaction with my open eyes when I utter these three most holy words to you. I wanted to see that faithfulness in your eyes, I wanted to feel that carefulness of yours from my heart, I wanted to be touched by your soft hands and wanted to feel the same warmth when by mistake or intentionally I touched you when I was with you.

I can feel the magnetic impact of such touches. Even today, I wanted to feel similarly when I am going to utter these words to you. But now, I have already been overcome by all sorts of emotions, feelings, and touches.

Now the only thing which I can feel in my body are these piercing needles, the intravenous drips and other life-saving machines which are counting my breath, which can anytime announce its final decision.

But now I have realized the only thought which kept me alive so long even though I am completely prepared for this moment, is the thought of you. Until I let you know about this fact, I could not achieve peace for my soul, for which I have fought so long.

Yes, my dear…my beloved…my darling… I LOVE YOU… and I loved you a lot from the moment I started knowing you, but this is my fear or weakness and the forcefulness of this moment, which never allowed me to mention it to you before. I had to run away from you the day you uttered those words tome. Sincerely speaking those were the best moments of my life. I can still feel those words of yours in my ear like you are whispering them right in front of me.

You see how helpless I am, who has everything in my life – faithful love, caring family and success in a short span but one thing which I am missing is time. But trust me, whatever time I have spent with you is like an eternity. You filled every moment with immense pleasure. Therefore now I am leaving without any complaint. The moment you have the scarcity of something, you realize its value, and for that, I thanked God that he sent you to make me feel so important in my own eyes.

You know, Satya, for me the definition of love is something very different. For me, it's just not the attraction or sex thing. It's not like living our whole life together and to achieve oneness in your life. For me, it's a compelling and divine thing. It's the power which drives your energy in a particular direction to accomplish your objective. If love leads to dilemma and confusion, then trust me, it's flawed. I know from the deep core of my heart that my love is not imperfect. You have to prove it to me, which I know you will.

I want to create so much value in this world that this whole world praises me. Promise me, Satya, now you will do that for me. One day you will achieve the most significant achievement of your life and create so much value to the world that this whole world will praise you. That day, you will find me standing next to you. This is my dream, which I want you to fulfil. Once again, I want to see this world from your eyes.

I wish I could keep writing, but I have already said whatever I wanted to say; now nothing is left. As it is stated that you come with empty hands and empty thoughts, and you have to leave like this only to rest in peace. There is nothing you can take with you along except for the ideas, and now I am relieved from that too.

It's not a goodbye but a welcome party for your bright future… so once again, let's have a party tonight.

Your love,

Preha.

15

That Togetherness

When I was in the middle of my in-depth thought process, Satya placed his hand on my shoulder. I looked at him. His face now seemed to be relaxed and calm, but still, I could see a hell of a lot of pain in his eyes. Such pain was justified too. After all, he had just lost his girlfriend forever, but to my relief, he had started talking.

"Hey, Satya… you proposed to her… wow, and you never told us… How mean? I always thought we all were fast friends, such that we share each and everything, but now I feel like everybody has his own story and everybody is hiding it from others for one or another reason."

"Shants… we really are good friends and trust me, I never tried to hide anything from anybody. You have seen how Rajiv tried to offend her. I don't want to listen or defend her in any way because I know what she was for me. This is the reason I kept quiet."

"Yeah, I can understand. But now why don't you tell me that proposal day story? I know the sort of bond you shared with her and how much you liked her."

"Shants… you know that was a gorgeous day and I must say it was a very auspicious one too. Also, that was a day full of religious and devotional feelings. That was the day of Ganesh Chaturthi. She called me up to her flat for the very first time. In fact, I believe from the male breed, I was the first one who had been invited to her flat.

"When I reached there, she opened the door. The moment I saw her, I desperately wanted to hug her. She was wearing a red and green combination traditional classic suit. Her neatly tied up long hair was nicely hooked to the clip behind and was falling flawlessly to the front over her shoulder, but was tucked behind her ears in a way that her diamond earrings were clearly visible and twinkling like two small stars. It appeared like a few of her hairs, though, refused to follow the path. They were covering her eyes and stuck to her lips. I wanted to lift my hand and tuck them behind like the others, but I couldn't dare to touch her.

"Her big, dramatic eyes, nicely beautified with light *surma*, appeared like river Ganga flowing flawlessly from the Himalayas, full of devotion and love. Her face was adorned with very light makeup. Above all, a small but bright smile was glued to her lips embellished with light pink lipstick and gloss. For the first time, I saw her that way. Stunned, I was looking at her and then she finally held my hand and dragged me inside with a sarcastic comment, *'Ab kab tak muje aise niharte rahoge, andar bhi aa jao?'*

(Until what time will you look at me like this, now why don't you come in.)

"Her one-room flat was nicely decorated like her only. In one corner of the drawing-room, a small temple was beautifully ornamented where along with other Hindu deities; Lord Ganesha was on a *chawki* under which a beautiful *rangoli* was drawn with two *sathiyas*. One was made of yellow and another was red, with opposite outlining with two *diyas* placed on each. They were like two giant welcome gates through which Lord Ganesha in person had passed and left his footmarks behind.

"Then she was religiously performing prayer. I was startled to see the in-depth knowledge she had of every tradition and with every act, she was explaining the reason behind it to me. After she was done with all the rituals, we stopped for a coffee break. She served me with all the delicious dishes she had prepared and what to tell about those dishes, Shants. I've never had such delicious food in my life and then only I came to know that she was an excellent cook too.

"After that, we left for Ganpati *Visarjan*. We took an auto-rickshaw to Juhu beach. By the time we reached the shore, it was all orange. The sun was almost going to draw in water, and its rays were spread in the water like gold particles dispersed all over there.

"There were a lot of devotees who were doing Ganpati *Visarjan* over there and chanting "*Ganpati Bappa Moriya, agle baras jaldi aana*" but she was silent. She was only smiling like she was capturing all the excitement within her.

"Oh… My… GOD!!! Shants…

"How damn stupid I was? She was giving me every indication, and I could not understand it. Now I can link her each and every activity".

"Shants…"

I could see the flow of emotion in Satya. Every time and with every incident it was changing. Sometimes it was excitement; sometimes a broad smile. Sometimes it was full of pain and sorrow, but in the end, I could see a deep peace within him, which had come from the sense of realization.

"When we reached the seashore, the *pooja thali* was in my hand. She stopped for a while and draped her *dupatta* on her head like the other women. Then she took the *thali* from me. We approached the sea.

"When we were in the water until our knees, she stopped. Probably she was afraid of going ahead. I went a little more forward, slightly bent down and did the Ganpati *Visarjan*. While doing so, I shouted '*Ganpati Bappa Moria. Agle baras fir aana*'.

"But she was silent, looking towards me like telling me that Ganpati will come again, but she won't be standing there anymore with me. The orange rays of the sun were directly falling on her. Due to the brisk wind, her *dupatta* had slid down from her head. Now her hair and *dupatta* were blowing in the wind.

"Shants, I can't tell you how beautiful, stunning and amazing she was looking at that time, like we were not on earth but standing in heaven. She was the most beautiful

Apsara of there. I continuously looked towards her. I wish that moment could remain still for forever.

"I approached her. When I was almost next to her, I could see that tears were flowing from her eyes, but before I could say anything, she quickly turned. She wiped off her tears, but I could feel the wetness in her eyes. I kept my hand on her shoulder and asked her. "What happened? But she didn't answer and let the moment pass. She held my hand, and we started walking on the beach.

"We walked on the beach for a long time, hand in hand, and she never tried to pull it out from my side. We walked until it was completely dark and then…"

Satya stopped for a while and then I could see the sorrow had again assailed him and to continue the momentum, I said, "… And that was the moment when you proposed to her."

Satya nodded. "Yes, Shants. That was the moment I proposed to her. I stopped for a while. I held both her hands in mine and pulled her so close to me that we were almost hugging each other.

"Preha… I love you… and I love you a lot and want to be together with you all the time. Do you like me? Will you marry me?

"She was startled. For a moment, she smiled as if she was going to say that she loved me, but instead of that, suddenly, pain floated into her eyes and the tears were back, like asking me *why did you say that? Why did you want to tease me and tear apart all my happiness?* She let go of my hands, turned and started running. I watched her running until she disappeared. That was the last time I saw her. Then I couldn't understand her feelings, but now I know what her actions meant…" With that, Satya started crying again and I did not stop him.

16
Finally I Called Her

3.00 AM

I didn't remember what I was thinking about until Satya stopped sobbing. Might be it was about love, hate, life, death, the universe or some stupid events. I just could not recall.

Finally, Satya interrupted my thought process and asked, "Did she call you?"

I said yes and told him the series of incidents.

"Okay… now what is your plan?"

"Plan… nothing as such."

"Did you call her back? Maybe she was waiting for you."

"No, I didn't. I didn't dare to. It was too late to call a girl at night."

"In love, there is nothing called early or late. You should call her now. Are you sure what life has planned next for you? So, why do you want to wait? Call her now."

"But I am not sure of her number, and I can't call on the landline. Maybe that number belonged to her brother or father, and she managed to get it for a while."

"Then, in that case, you see you are pretty safe. You can simply excuse yourself and can say you dialled a wrong number mistakenly."

"But by now she would have slept… I will call in the morning."

"But what if she is waiting for you? Again, if you call her in the morning, there's a fair chance that the same story gets repeated. Don't you worry, dial right now, Shants."

I got a little inspiration and motivation from him. Even I didn't want to wait until morning.

I called on the number from which I had received a call from her. It rang for a long time. Finally, I heard a sleepy voice. Probably it was on silent mode but on vibration and kept nearby, and due to the vibration, the lady woke up.

The moment I heard a hello from the lady, I realized it was not her. If it was not her, who was it? Was she her mother or sister, I was not able to guess?

She asked, "Who is calling?"

I couldn't answer her question. I didn't dare to.

She again asked the same question, but this time her voice was crystal clear. She waited for a moment, and then she said, "Are you mad that you call at such a weird hour and now you're not speaking at all."

I tried to speak, but out of fear, I didn't dare to speak. My whole body was sweating by now. I could just whisper.

The voice waited for a moment. When she was not sure of my whispering words, suddenly she asked in a sharp voice, "Is that Shantilal? How boring and typical your name is!"

In a choked voice, I said, "Yes."

"But now it seems you are a fool too, but I like your style. At least you dared to call at such a weird hour but then, what took you so long to call back?"

"Sorry, I know I am such a fool, but you see sometimes we are bound by circumstances not to adhere to the schedules and today, it was my bad luck that I got stuck in such events."

"Oh, is it? Now if you don't mind, would you let me know what those are?"

I briefed her about the events. Then I politely asked her if she could reveal her identity now.

"I am her sister." Except for buttering and pleasing her, I was not left with any other option. Finally, she said, "It's okay this time but next time, mind you." And then I heard her sarcastic voice, "*Oye le... Aa gaya tere majnu ka* call." (Hello, your Majnu has called you).

And finally, I heard the voice of my love- Aaisha. It was so sweet, like honey, and then eventually we had a conversation. Now I don't remember what we talked about. We spoke of day or night, light or dark, the sun or moon or about our personal and professional lives, about hobbies and many more things like any other romantic couple talk for the first time. It was nothing different from others, but the most important thing was that after so much effort, we finally talked.

I told her about all the incidents that had happened and what efforts we had made to reach her, and she laughed and laughed endlessly, and I too was laughing with her. All the pain of waiting, all the sorrow of missing and all the fear of losing had been washed away and what lay ahead was excitement and happiness. Nothing more and nothing less.

I didn't realize when the sun's rays started falling on me, and for the first time, I felt the morning of exciting Mumbai; by now it was 6 AM. The heart still wanted to talk a lot, but after three hours of talk, we had to stop, and her sister's small communication device was mediated as a source of my love.

She told me about the story of that device too. Her father gave both of them a choice, to opt for one thing - a Kinetic bike or a mobile. As usual, her sister was smarter; she chose the mobile, and she was left with the bike.

So in this way, finally, a new love story had started. Another 'Heer-Ranjha', 'Laila-Majnu'… whatever you call it… had been created, but like all other love stories, this story had its own twists and turns, its own excitement, its own pain, and sorrow and like any story, either such a tale has a happy or sad ending; mine too has an end. Now let's see what it was. As of now, I leave it to your wild guesses. What could it be? Joy or sorrow… the following pages will tell.

When I was done with my call, I looked for Satya, but he was not there. Where the hell had he gone? Just to avoid doubts about any unfortunate event, I looked down, but I didn't see any movement and ran downstairs. To my horror, I didn't find Satya in the flat too. I woke everybody up, and we all had only one question in our mind, "Where the hell has Satya gone?" And I could see Kamal was looking towards me disappointed.

Part 11

17

My Caring Boss

"Shants… I trusted you…" Kamal's voice appeared disheartened, but before he could complete his sentence, Rajiv cried in anger, "Damn it!! His phone too is switched off."

"Friends! Please don't worry. I know where he must have gone." I told them the complete story about his proposal, his last meeting with her, and by the time I finished it, we saw Satya enter the flat. We all were relieved to see him. We started our day to day routines. After such a long and hectic night though, the heart was not allowing us to go to the office; still, we overruled our heart and went to work. After all, it was our first job. We all were in the first six months of work and entirely dedicated to our jobs.

Though I was tired due to a sleepless night filled with surprises, I didn't know from where I got so much energy. I was very enthusiastic about my work. Probably this is what happens in love. You automatically feel excited.

Hold on. Did I tell you that what my profile in office was? I was responsible for ensuring that all the receivables collected as money by various modes, especially cheques, are appropriately accounted for, deposited into the bank, realized, and the funds are available for claim settlements and investments. In other words 'mere reconciliation'. Anyway, that was my first job, and I loved it no matter how much I despised it later.

I quickly reviewed my to-do list for the day, completed the initial reviews, estimated and submitted a budget for the day, gave the necessary instructions to my subordinates, Rajesh and Dhawal, and finally, when everything was over, I arched back my body into the chair. The beauty of the chair was that it adjusted itself according to my wish. But before I could think of Aaisha for a moment primarily, and before I could think of my delicious lunch, which my empty stomach was craving for secondly, my manager came rushing in. Before I could speak, he bombarded me with his usual tone.

"Shantilal, *mere dost… Aaj to lag raha hai chaddi fat kar hi rahegi.*" (Shantilal, today is the day of crisis.)

I quickly jumped out of my chair. "Why what happened, sir?" I quizzed him.

"We have a review first thing in the morning tomorrow at 9 AM with the Operations head. First, gather the entire team." In no time, the entire team was in front of us.

My manager who was fair, slim and short but with a perpetually worried face and always a yes man to the management, had in no time quickly become head of the entire Accounts operations. No doubt unexpected quick success had gone to his head and made him a bit arrogant too. He pretended to be humble with the team on the face, but behind our backs, he used to badmouth each one of us with another team member during smoke or tea breaks. He always made us swear that we do not share it with anybody no matter what. What he didn't realize was that we five musketeers (out of seven) were sharing the same flat and didn't hide anything from each other. So we knew very well what he was up to always.

He announced, "We have to prepare a presentation by 4 PM. Then I will review along with the national manager in the evening at 6 PM. Prepare something so that we can edit it by 8 PM." But he never told us what the review was about and what he wanted to present.

We were back in our seats and started preparing. By 4 PM we gathered again, but he didn't like any of the slides we'd made. He gave some instructions. We were back to work. By 6 PM, we gathered again and once more, he didn't like the slides though they were prepared according to his instructions. He ran into the national manager. After an hour, he came back frowning.

He gathered the team and announced that whatever we had prepared till then was all crap. He loathed us, but the loathing was mutual. We didn't like it that the asshole was not yet clear as to what he wanted to present and was yelling at us.

At 9 PM, again we modified the slides as per the instructions provided. He quickly reviewed them along with the national manager. He seemed to be a bit satisfied, but he wanted to include more information on the amount of premium collected, the cheque bounced details, the status of policy to money and money to policy reconciliation, how we monitor high-value cheques, aspects of operating agents working, number of business collected at the branch, etc.

Despite all the system challenges, we prepared the slides by midnight. The presentation was now running up to a total of 50 slides, but he still was not happy with the formatting of the slides so finally, he sat by himself, reviewing each business area, discussing, formatting, modifying and discarding a few slides. He was sitting at his desk while we were standing around him. Needless to say, in between, we were taking smoking or tea breaks. We were cribbing about his intelligence, unpreparedness and wondering what would happen at the meeting. It was supposed to be an hour-long meeting but looking at the presentation, it seemed like it was going to run the entire day.

At 4 AM, finally, he finished and closed his laptop. He stretched his arms; though we could still see the dissatisfaction on his face he managed to send the final presentation to the national manager for his early morning review.

In the meantime, Aaisha called me twice. I explained to her about how stressful the situation was. She understood, and we talked very briefly during our tea or smoking breaks. Since the night had already drifted away in slides and smoke, we decided to go home, take a quick nap and be back in the office by 8 AM.

We reached the office at sharp 8 AM, but there was no sign of our boss. We kept waiting until 8.30 AM. Finally, we saw the national manager approaching us. He was short and disfigured but always had a smile on his face. We were aghast to hear that our boss had left us in the lurch. He was not coming because he'd fallen sick. We were now on our own to present to our operations head.

We were not sure what was going to happen next, but for sure we could feel butterflies in our stomach. Our feet were trembling in fear and in anticipation of the outcome of the meeting.

Yes, that was my first boss who was my so-called God.

My first mentor, my first adventure in the corporate world.

Sometimes it sucks, sometimes it motivates one to take the plunge into something new.

18

I Made a Plan to Meet Her

We all were sitting in a conference room with a mahogany table at the centre, equipped with all modern facilities like a big screen on one hand and a whiteboard on the other. That was our first formal interaction with our operations head. While we were looking at each other bemused, our operations head entered the room. He was tall, fit, with a glowing face and slightly grey hair.

In a couple of seconds, he settled himself. "Okay, what are we reviewing today?"

As soon as presentation flashed on the big screen, we started seeing the disappointment on our operations head's face, and our hearts began sinking too. After flipping the slides for a while, the operation head announced, "Cut this crap. All I wanted was a simple process overview and the challenges we are facing and known identified issues which we want to highlight to our internal auditors, but it seems what you are presenting over here are mere facts which I know very well." Without further disappointing us, he said, "I acknowledge all the hard work you have put in preparing this presentation together, but this is not what I want. I want each one of you to stand up and give me a brief on your process, challenges faced and any self-identified issues that need my attention and which we can highlight to the auditor. That's it! So now, who is going first?" We all could see last night's efforts going down the drain.

I stood up and started speaking. Inside I was nervous, but I tried to appear confident. I said in a stammering voice, "Sir if you do not mind, may I use the board to show you the process flow?"

He shrugged in approval. I quickly drew the entire process flow which I was handling and circled the known identified issue. Above all, I made it very clear that at any given point of time, 5% of the outstation cheques remain un-reconciled/un-realizable due to various problems like a mismatch in entries, distant corporation banks in villages and clearing issues.

After that, everybody similarly presented their area and now our operation head seemed to be satisfied. Within two hours our presentation was over. We all felt relieved, including our national manager. Our immediate boss remained unaware of the details of the meeting. He did not make any real attempts to know what had really happened at the meeting except for a cursory overview as he was sure it was meant to be a meeting where we would get bashed and was very confident about the adverse outcome.

Since I was drained that day due to continued lack of sleep for two consecutive days, I took early leave from the office and headed back home. When I reached home, my father called, informing me that my sister's wedding date was scheduled for 9th February. He wanted me to arrive home no later than 5th February. I was not sure why he was insisting on 5th February, but I guessed I was needed to help with the wedding preparations. After all, it was my one and only sister's wedding. This good news excited me, and I cooked up a plan to meet Aaisha…

In my excitement, I quickly informed my boss informally about the leave I needed and the next day itself, I applied it into the system. I called her up. I told her about my plan, that I would reach Jaipur by flight first thing in the morning from Mumbai. We would have the whole day to spend time with each other, and finally, in the evening, I would leave for my hometown, Bharatpur.

She seemed to be equally excited, and with great zeal, we both were waiting eagerly for the fateful day when we would meet again, but this time as love birds.

19

The Fateful Day

It was my first date, and for the first date you can imagine how well you want to be prepared for it. Especially when you are living with your friends; even if you want to look at it like a typical day, they won't allow it to happen. Plans were made, a gift was decided upon, hang-out places were being explored in Jaipur on Google, but you know what, no matter how well you want to plan, the beauty of the first date is, it always follows its own pace, and the same thing happened with me. Not to mention that here I was dying to meet Aaisha, there she too was waiting eagerly.

My flight to Jaipur was scheduled at 6 AM in the morning on 4th February, but the flight got delayed by two hours. I had initially thought that I would first go to my cousin's place and then after changing, I would meet her at 11 AM at our decided place. Instead, I had to go there directly now, but as I said, in such cases, things never work the way we plan.

I reached Jaipur's Sanganer airport at 10 AM. As soon as I exited the plane, cold winter breeze hit my face, and I could feel the difference in temperature between Mumbai and Jaipur. Though it was a cold sunny day it was the most romantic day in my life.

In those days, we didn't have smartphones. I had a basic keypad Nokia phone, so there was no option to WhatsApp. As soon as I came out of the airport, I messaged her. Within a few minutes, I got a reply from her that the plan needed to be changed as her father was not going to the office but out of town due to some work at 1 PM. She needed to drop him at Gandhi Nagar station. So she would not be able to leave before that. I messaged her mentioning that 1 PM was perfectly all right with me too.

Thankfully, I got some time to rest and refresh myself, which I badly needed as I had not slept the whole night, first as I got back very late from office, secondly due to the flight and thirdly because of the excitement. On my way to my cousin's place, who lived in Jawahar Nagar, I was looking out of the cab continuously and was mesmerized, maybe by the beauty of the pink city or maybe everything appeared to be so beautiful as I was going to meet my love for the first time as a lover. On top of it, the cab driver had turned on the radio, which was playing the most romantic songs ever. So what I was feeling at that time, I could hardly imagine now.

After reaching my cousin's place, I took a quick nap and freshened up. I gulped down the breakfast she had offered me. I left from her home at around 12.30 PM. She called me and said she was at Gandhi Nagar station and that our decided meeting place, Jawahar Circle, was in the opposite direction so it would be better to choose a new meeting place. When nothing came to my mind, I quickly said, "Birla Mandir." She chuckled but agreed, and later on, I cursed myself for fixing a date at a temple. Anyway, what was done couldn't be undone as it meant more delay, which I could not afford anymore.

I reached Birla Mandir at sharp 1 PM. I waited for her. Every single moment was making me more anxious. My whole body was shivering in excitement. I was excitedly waiting for her. I was looking for every single red Maruti 800 bearing the nameplate RJ14CA0044. See I still remember the number of the car even though it is long gone and has been replaced. Though that car had a lot more memories connected with it. Finally, the moment came. Time started moving in languid motion. My heart started beating much faster, imagining how she would appear in my wildest dreams. When the car stopped in front of me, first the door opposite the driver opened and my gaze moved there. First out came the left leg in a shining silver stiletto, then appeared her long dark hair flying in the cold wind and finally, she materialized, as if straight from heaven, like an angel attired in a light white and pink suit, wearing a sweet smile on her face. I was utterly astonished and gazed at her without blinking or uttering a single word. My attention was broken by her sister's voice; she appeared from the driver's seat playing gooseberry. She winked at me. "Hey. Will you both keep staring at each other like this or should I say something?" I was brought back to earth from heaven by this third wheel, and I grinned, "Hey! How are you?"

She approached me smiling, and she asked, "Now what's the plan?"

I stuttered for a while but quickly gained control of my voice. I looked around. I saw an elderly woman selling flowers along with *pooja thalis*. I approached her, leaving both of them puzzled. I grabbed a *pooja thali* and uttered, "Now, when we are in the footsteps of miraculous Ganpati *Bappa*, why not take blessing from him first? It will give a good start to our relationship." She smiled, and we all three approached the Ganpati temple.

After taking blessings from God, I was craving for tea, but it seemed cheap to go to a roadside *tapri* on my first date. I said, "Why don't we go to CCD?"

"Yeah! Sounds good." Her sister grinned again, winking, but this time at her sister. When we reached the car, her sister automatically got into the driver's seat. Of course, she sat next to her, and I was in the back seat. Then I quizzed, "Don't you know how to drive?"

"Of course I do, but if she wants to be the driver, I don't mind."

"I don't buy it," I said, shrugging my shoulders.

"Okay, now let me show you." While saying this, she jumped out of the car. They both quarrelled for a while, but after a lot of insisting and instigating from my side, finally, her sister gave in. She jumped into the back seat, and of course, now I was in the front seat next to her.

She ignited the engine, and soon the car was flying. "Slow down," her sister cried. "No need to show off. I love my life even if you don't." She didn't care. In fact, she increased the speed and jumped two signals. At the third one, she halted the car with screeching tires. If I were not wearing a seatbelt, I would have definitely bumped into the dashboard. Her sister had almost fallen down from her seat. "Wowww!" I exclaimed. For the rest of the drive, her sister and I were holding our breath and praying. Finally, we reached our destination, and we breathed a deep sigh of relief.

At CCD, I ordered a cappuccino for myself, two café frappes for them, along with cookies and sandwiches for munching. Her sister seemed to be in haste, pretending that her friend was calling. She quickly escaped along with her frappe and cookies but chuckled, "You've got a lot of money." She instructed her sister that she would be back in another hour and a half, so to remain at CCD only.

After a long time, for which I had been waiting eagerly, we were left alone. I don't remember what we talked about, but in a while, we both started feeling suffocated in CCD. Finally, she proposed we go to Jawahar Circle. This time she drove smoothly without jumping any signal.

It was 4 PM. Sunrays managed to escape behind the clouds, and winter winds suddenly started blowing a bit harder. While getting out of the car, she put on her jacket, stretching her hands out. A sudden desire arose within me to hug her; however, I stopped my urge. I approached her so carefully that I could feel the warmth of her breath. She suddenly wrapped herself with her arms. Her hair started blowing on to her face like cloudy nights play with the moon.

I carefully extended my hands towards her face and pushed her hair behind her ear carefully. I believe she understood my next move, so she quickly stepped back. She grabbed my hand and started walking towards the most beautiful garden I had ever seen. Hand in hand, our fingers tingling and playing with each other, we took a leisurely walk around the circle. The crowd started to thin due to the cold, but we were feeling much warmer side by side. I appreciated the privacy and the walk.

We reached the centre of a large circle where there was a small rose garden. A variety of roses was blossoming, making the environment more romantic. This time, I could not resist the urge and I held her soft cheeks in my palms. This time she did not resist. My heart started pounding rapidly. Every part of my body could feel the thrill. Her eyes closed automatically, like she too was enjoying the way I was. As soon as I touched her pink rosy lips with mine, out of nowhere, a gardener appeared and shouted, "Time is over." He gave us stern looks. She was so abashed that she quickly ran away. I too was feeling embarrassed but maintained my composure and briskly walked towards her car.

Before she started the engine, she reached towards the back seat. She grabbed a paper bag. "I brought something for you." I opened the bag. I found a card and a small teddy bear in it, which was very cute. "Where is my gift?"

"Oh God! I shall be truthful with you. I had decided the gift for you, but yesterday I was late from the office. When I reached the nearby shop, I couldn't find it. Also, I didn't find anything worthy for you. I did not have time to explore the other shops. But wait a minute now, I know what is worthy for you." I quickly got out of the car and ran to the rose garden situated in the centre of the circle where the gardener was still wandering, but I didn't care two hoots for him. I grabbed a red rose and started running before the gardener could even react. Finally, I reached the car where she was waiting impatiently. "Where were you?"

"Here, this is for you."

"Oh, how cheap but I love your choice."

While plucking it, a little thorn had pricked my finger, and blood oozed out. She noticed it and bandaged it with her small handkerchief. A low price paid for beauty but only God knows what other prices I would need to pay ahead.

She dropped me at GT again at 5 PM. I said goodbye, pecking her cheek, and that was the end of my first beautiful date. I watched her leaving while holding my cheek and smiling. Nothing had gone as per schedule, but everything that had happened was spellbinding.

20

The Revolt

On the same evening, I left for my hometown cherishing all the memories of that romantic day. When I reached home, I fell asleep as soon as I hit the sofa in the drawing-room. It was due to lack of sleep for consecutive days. My mother didn't disturb me but lovingly covered me up on the sofa itself. I slept until 8 AM. I woke up when my mother scolded me, "Get up! There are guests at home."

I woke up rubbing my eyes as if had I landed in an unknown zone. While I was getting ready, my parents were busy entertaining guests at home. Finally, my father called me. I appeared in the drawing room again. I found two men sitting across the room. Both were dark but one had a stern face and the other was grinning. "Ah! Here he is," my father said. They asked me a couple of questions like an interview being conducted by an interviewer. After some time, they took leave. Iwas confused but got a hint of what was happening. I waited until they left, then quizzed my father what it was about. He said they were looking for a groom for their daughter.

"Is this the reason you were insisting on my arriving by the 5th?" I asked.

"Yes, of course. That was the plan."

"But you had not told me earlier."

"I know the answer that is why I did not tell. Also, we should talk about such things face to face and not on the phone."

"My answer is still the same as I am not ready."

"I am not going to hear this. You are 26 and ready to take the plunge. I am not insisting on the same girl. First, meet and decide. I am very well aware of this family. That guy is my childhood friend and financial advisor to the finance minister."

"So what? I need to marry her daughter not him."

"Here is the daughter's biodata and her snap. Have a look at it. She is pursuing an MBA. She will get a job soon."

I didn't care to look at it and announced my final decision, "I am not ready for marriage, and I will not do it now."

"I know the answer, but I am not listening to you. I have already committed to my friend. You are going to meet his daughter tomorrow…"

Before he finished the sentence, I rushed out from the room but I knew very well that he would not leave any stone unturned to make it happen. But this time even I was not ready to give in. At the same time, it would be too early to tell him about Aaisha. There was no further discussion about it the entire day. I knew my father would not let it go like this. The whole day I remained busy with my sister's wedding arrangements. The whole day, my sister kept teasing and provoking me, "You got me hooked. Now it's my turn to get you trapped." I kept avoiding her.

My sister, who was 22, had just finished college after pursuing her Masters in classical music. She was tall, splendid and attractive. Since she was the only sister of two brothers, we adored her a lot. Initially, she did not agree to the marriage. Even I was not convinced, considering her age, and wanted her to study further and complete her PhD, but it was again my father who made the entire plan.

He visited the groom's place with one of my uncles for his daughter. Somehow their plan could not be fructified because of *Kundli's*, as they didn't reconcile, which is a mandatory requirement in India. I would say this is the fourth condition of marriage in India. The three conditions are rightly mentioned by bestselling author Chetan Bhagat, "In India, marriage is a three-step process. The boy's family must like the girl's family, the girl's family must like the boy's family, and finally, the boy and girl must love each other."

My uncle, who was my math's teacher as well as a mentor to me in my school days, suggested my father, "If it is not working out for me why don't you try for your daughter?"

My father was fascinated by the idea. As he liked the groom's family, without wasting any more time, he made a plan. Though I opposed it fiercely, he used my uncle as a shield. As he was my mentor, I had no choice but to listen to him. Even my sister didn't like the idea, but she didn't oppose directly as she had utmost faith in me. She knew that I would not budge from my decision in any scenario. But you know what, couples are made in heaven, and if it is already fated, then you are bound to meet, come what may, and that's exactly what happened in my sister's case. I didn't like the idea, but the circumstances were such that I had to give up.

Our uncle had provided comfort to us that it would happen informally. My sister and I reached our uncle's place at a scheduled time where the groom's parents were waiting for us already. The moment they met my sister, they were so excited that they immediately proposed for fixing the date of the wedding. They called their son who was staying in Bhiwadi. Meanwhile, my sister was staring at me in discomfort, and I just shrugged.

Uncle understood our dilemma. He took the initiative to calm down the groom's father and said, "Since he is here until this week let him visit Bhiwadi and meet your son, and if they agree, then we will make the next plan."

Next day I reached Bhiwadi along with my cousin. We were waiting for him to arrive at the bus stand. Suddenly a bike stopped, screeching in front of us. I was amazed to see that the guy who was in front of me was Hemant. He was my friend's friend and I knew him very well. Hemant was sophisticated, well-mannered and above all, a terrific looking and fit guy. Though there was a five-year gap between Hemant and my sister, I could not find a single reason for not agreeing to the match and finally I gave in. From that day on, my sister called me a deserter.

Considering those scenarios, I knew my father would not remain quiet. He would definitely plan something for me too but that time was different, and no love was involved. In my case, how could I betray my love?

In the evening, I understood his plot. Arvind uncle and his wife came home. My father knew very well that I could let him down but not my uncle. He was a lecturer of Accountancy and a tenant in our house since my childhood. He got married in our home. Aunty became my favourite, and the love was mutual. Later on, when we grew up, they moved, but I used to spend more time in their house than mine. Since he was an accounts lecturer, he had a significant influence on my career too. He was my mentor since childhood; he had influenced me a lot more than my father. There is no way he would let me procrastinate on anything. He always used convincing arguments to make me do what he wanted.

Finally, in a closed room, when uncle and aunty talked to me, I told them that I was in love with a girl in Jaipur, and that was the primary reason for my not wanting to get married. I told them we had met once. In fact, I was not even aware of her father's name and where they came from. Uncle asked me to call Aaisha and get the details of her family background. After that, he would talk to my father.

I called her immediately and let her know about the situation I was facing. She was facing a similar situation at her home too, but she too had not disclosed anything about us to her parents. She was not aware that her father had gone to Bharatpur, which was their ancestral place. He had asked her to come to Bharatpur the next morning along with her sister, mother, and brother. We both were worried, but I was confident that with uncle by my side, I had a chance to win this battle.

I said, "What a coincidence that we are facing a similar situation simultaneously and you and your entire family is going to be in my hometown. It will be much easier to manage."

I let uncle know all the details. Then my uncle talked to my father in private. I was sure he would convince him but to my surprise, when they called me in, my father said, "Since we have already committed to them, we should go and see her at least once to keep our word. Later on, we always have the choice to say no."

"But uncle, why this drama? We are not some articles in the museum. Are we? We can simply say that I am already in love and cannot visit the mysterious man's place."

"We have listened to you, and now you must listen to us. There is no harm in visiting your father's friend's place once. This is very common in our society. Nobody will think otherwise if you say no to this relationship. After that, we will talk to Aaisha's parents too. Now we have their number and details as well," my uncle said.

Frustrated, I agreed, and it was decided that along with my sister, uncle and aunty, we would visit the mysterious man's place at 3 PM.

I called Aaisha and informed her, and she told me that she would inform her family too about us and we both agreed that come what may, we would not allow our love story to end this way.

21

The Mysterious Man's Place

I called her first thing in the morning. She was already on the way to Bharatpur. We both had butterflies in our stomachs, but we tried to comfort each other and decided that we would maintain our composure during the day. I said, "In the evening, I will ask my uncle to call your father and hopefully, everything will be fine by then."

"What if things don't work out the way we want?" she asked.

"I will not allow it to happen like that. Have you talked to your mother?" I said.

"Not yet but I will before reaching Bharatpur. I am sure I can convince my father to at least have a word with your father once before finalizing anything."

"Okay! Take care. I have to go. I've got a lot of arrangements to be completed for my sister's marriage. Everything will be all right. Don't you worry," I said and cut the line.

Meanwhile, I was stuck with my own dilemma. I got a call from my office. It was my boss on the line.

"Hey, Shants! Sorry to disturb you on leave but this auditor is asking for data for audit for the last six months. I got the data from the team, but I can still see some un-reconciled items in the data".

"Yeah, sir that is the fact. We have explanations for each item."

"Yeah, *dost* but in tens of thousands of data what impact will 70 lines items create? There is no way an auditor can find them out. Let's delete them and send the data to the auditor. What do you think?"

"Sir, as you deem fit. You have better experience in audits."

"Okay then, let's remove it and send it to that prick. I know this auditor intentionally picked my area because she is after me and jealous of me. She is good for nothing and should be fired immediately."

"As you like, sir."

"How is the marriage preparation going on?"

"All good, sir."

"You must be busy. Catch you later, bye." And he cut the line. I did not give any further thought to this as I was struggling with my own burning issue.

At the scheduled time, we reached the stranger's place. Deep inside, in my heart, I was disgusted at the prospect of two persons being made to appear like exhibition pieces.

He warmly welcomed us and settled us in their drawing room, and the Indian marriage drama began.

Hundreds of delicious items including sweets and *namkeen* were being served with tea, coffee and juice. I was gazing at my sister, and she shrugged and signalled me to maintain my calm.

After a lot of chattering and a detailed interview with me, the time had come for the entry of the heroine in the movie. As soon as she appeared with her sister in the room, I was stunned and remained open-mouthed. The *kajukatli* which I was about to gulp remained hanging in my hand. I froze on seeing her. My face changed colour and looking at me, my sister pinched me and scolded me, telling me to behave appropriately.

I was stunned not because she was as divinely beautiful as her name suggested, frozen not because she was more attractive than my love but because it was my love, my Aaisha, who was standing in front of me. For a moment I thought I was dreaming and in an alien world and then I asked my sister to pinch me once more.

Aaisha was smiling at me, and once again, she appeared more beautiful than ever in a pink saree. My uncle grinned. "Shocked to hell and what do you think, only you can play tricks and not us?" With this, a burst of laughter broke in the room, and the only two people who were abashed were Aaisha and me.

"As and when you told us about her family background, we immediately realized it was the same girl you were talking about, but we maintained the suspense," my uncle said.

I said, "But I have a request. Though we love each other, still we need some time to be prepared for the next step of our life. At least a year to be well prepared."

"Even we are not in a hurry and want her to finish her MBA first," her father said. Our wedding was finalized for a year later. Finally, it was a happy ending for the next beginning.

Confused? Aren't you? You are wondering what the hell is going on. So let me clarify - it was the same girl whom I loved so much and married. Then after all that, what love have I been talking about till now? What caused us to fall apart that she had to leave me?

Yes, it was the same love, but it was the monotonous life after marriage that made us fall apart. As usual, people expect the experience to be more exciting after the wedding as compared to before marriage, but in our case, it became more mundane.

Earlier it was all about togetherness after all that struggle, but now it was all about understanding the aspirations of each other and becoming complementary in achieving the goals of life together. But somehow, instead of achieving the goals, we were drifting apart. Having a beautiful home along with a few middle-class luxuries - what you expect from a middle-class family - we had already got. You must be wondering what goals I am talking about; you will come to know in a short while.

22

Valentine's Day

Though it was my sister's wedding, I was the one who was the centre of attraction and the butt of ridicule. Finally, I was blissful and never imagined that God would make my revolt so simple that I didn't need to become a freedom fighter. My return flight was scheduled from Jaipur on 14th February at 7 PM and once again, I was happily destined to meet her but this time not clandestinely but officially as fiancé and fiancée.

This time, her home was our meeting place. Above all, this time I was not empty-handed but carried a gift selected by my parents. My father jeered, "Today is what youngsters called Valentine's Day, and you want to go empty-handed?" In India, Valentine's Day became famous not as a sign of love but more because it was perceived as an attack on Indian culture by the moral army. The first page of the newspaper in those days would always be covered with such news on the following day, and hence my father instructed me not to go to any secluded places and become an easy target of the moral army.

When I reached Jaipur, her father arrived at the bus stand to pick me up. As soon as I got down, he warmly welcomed me. As a sign of respect, I touched his feet. At the house, lavish snacks were waiting for me. I was introduced to her sister-in-law, Niti *Bhabhi* and little Arnav, with whom I cuddled the rest of the day. Though it was Valentine's Day for me, it was more of a family day.

We had lunch in a restaurant at GT. That was the only time we were left alone. I sneaked around and bought a bouquet of red roses for her. We wandered leisurely for a while at GT. Seeing the red roses in her hand, my dearest would-be *Sali* jeered, "Oho red roses and where are mine; because of me, you were able to meet."

I knew that was coming and hence I had already brought a small bouquet of pink roses for her too as a gesture of gratitude. It was because of her mobile that we were able to talk. It was now 5 PM, which meant our time to part had come. The airport was a 30-minute drive from GT. They dropped me at the airport, we said goodbye to each other. That was an emotional moment for me, and I could see her teary eyes. I wanted to hug her badly but couldn't do so in front of her family. I entered the airport for check-in.

As soon as I reached the flight counter, the attendant informed me that the flight had been preponed by 45 minutes to 6.15 PM. "That's a surprise for me!" I gasped.

"Didn't you receive the message, sir?" she asked politely.

I was still in time as the clock said it was 5.45 PM. She asked me to be quick and go ahead for security check.

When the security guy was checking me, his device made a loud beeping noise and then I realized that the gift which was meant for her, given by my father, was still in my jeans pocket.

"Holy shit!"

I told the security guy that this was supposed to be for my fiancée and I needed to call her quickly. First, he gave me a dirty look but then he called his colleague who was at the screening machine, "*Arre bhai ka mobile phone jara pass kar de. Yaha to Laila Majnu ka mamla hai.*" (Please handover his mobile. Here is a case of Laila-Majnu.) He smiled while handing over the phone to me.

I quickly called her and asked her to come back again as there was something important which I had missed. Luckily, she was just about to leave the airport, and hence her brother turned the car around. I reached out to the attendant and asked her to hold on for me.

"Sir! That's not possible. You will miss your flight. Boarding gates have been already opened."

But when I told her the story, she agreed but cautioned me to make it very quick. I ran towards the entry gate. I found her standing outside. I could see her puzzled face, but without wasting any more time, I handed her the gold chain that my father had asked me to gift her. I quickly hugged her and pecked her on her cheek and ran towards the security check-in. In the meantime, the final call was announced for me. A flight attendant helped me to pass through the security queue. The security guard rechecked me and stamped clearance, and I ran towards the boarding gate.

Thankfully, the boarding gate was still open for me. I breathed a sigh of relief. When I boarded the craft, my love called, thanking me for the gift and asking whether I had successfully boarded or not. In the meanwhile, the flight attendant asked me to switch off my mobile as the flight was about to take off. I followed her instructions and said goodbye to her.

I felt so relieved and so grateful to God that he had created one particular person for me who cared about me. I cried tears of joy, but only God knew how stressful the days ahead were going to be for me.

23

Those 70 Lines

When I reached home, my friends were excited to hear my story, but after we settled down, Abhishek who was directly working with our operations head gave me shocking news, "Shants! what the fuck have you done with the audit data?"

"What do you mean by that?" I fumed.

"I was in a management meeting where audit points were being discussed. When, at one place, the explanation was being asked on accounts receivable data, your boss said it's Shantilal who kept the file that way. Further explanation can only be provided when he is back, but I am telling you that it's going to be a very grave matter as management was seriously concerned about this particular point. So be careful of your actions when you reach office and better, I suggest you contact Sanchita first, our internal auditor, as she was looking for you,"Abhishek cautioned me.

I grunted, "I know this asshole will certainly create some mess, but anyway, let's talk in the office about it." I went to sleep thinking about my sweet memories of her.

The next day, when I reached the office, my boss lumbered towards me and made polite conversation. Within my heart, I was telling myself, knowing that he was not being upfront, "Come on prick, tell me what the hell, do you want from me?" He pointed towards the meeting room, and we both went there.

He said in a disgruntled manner, "The wretch had made a dire audit point on those 70 lines that were deleted from the file, and she is after us on that badly."

"But we had an explanation available for each of those lines and why it remained un-reconciled."

"I am sure you must have. That will be definitely required, but the point which was made is of data integrity." I could not think of anything, so I said that as a matter of fact, we maintain a separate file for the long-pending un-reconciled items from the main file for better monitoring and hence these items are not there."

"But that does not make sense, sir. How will we prove that?"

"I know, but we have to defend it somehow, else it will be a big issue to maintain the same status quo. I will take care of it, don't you worry. Actually speaking, that whore is good for nothing and when she didn't find anything in the audit, she made this a burning issue."

"I understand sir." And I thought, being savvy, he would be able to cook up some stories so it would be better to go by his story. After all, the boss is always right.

Stressed, I rummaged through the files and gathered all the explanations of each line item and gave them to him. But on the floor, the environment was such that I was looked at as the biggest culprit. That made me more stressed. I knew that by now he would have earwigged each one of them and made everybody feel that I was convicted and that he would act like a saviour for me.

I felt numb and due to anxiety, my whole body was sweating. Bharat *bhai* came to my rescue and took me for a tea break. He informed me that the matter was actually not that simple but far more complicated. He said, "Actually speaking his position is at stake and he will not leave a single stone unturned to put everything on you. I am sure you and your team will be called for further testimony by senior management. So better be careful and in fact, be very cautious. I would suggest you talk to Sanchita first as she was looking for you too." She was a close friend of Bharat *bhai* so he called her up and mentioned to her that we were outside and she could come and talk to me.

We met at a Café Coffee Day outside our office. She told me, "Shants! I know you are a perfect guy and you don't want to hurt anybody. Here it's not about hurting anybody but to remain truthful and I want you to say exactly what really happened. This is not the case of just 70 lines but about integrity. How did that asshole think he can give me some defunct data and imagine that I would never come to know about it? What he didn't realize is that I am in this company for the last five years and know every detail and the nitty-gritty of every process. As and when I saw that data and didn't see any un-reconciled item, immediately I knew something is goofed up here. Let me tell you that this case is very personal and I will highlight it to the management board of group companies and what slang does he use, *'kapde fat jayenge'*. So yes, this time I will make sure he will be standing nude in the market. So I suggest you don't come in between else you will be facing all the repercussions of this case and you will be fired. He will enjoy pretending he is standing by your side. So make your decision wisely. That's all I have to say."

"Isn't there a middle ground to it?" I asked sheepishly.

"I'm afraid not. As I said, it's a personal war, and I want to see that asshole out of this company." She shrugged and left for the office.

That night, I was very restless. I badly wanted some comfort and who else could give me better support than Aaisha? I called her at night and told her about the entire episode. She listened attentively and finally said, "What I really think is that you must listen to your heart and remain truthful."

"My heart really wants to quit now. I can't take this anymore."

"You may quit any time but if you quit now, you will be running away from your responsibilities. Also, you will be declared a criminal for this. The best time to quit anything is always when you are on the top, not at the bottom. In this scenario, you will be called a quitter. Do exactly what she said. Now calm yourself and sleep well. This too shall pass."

Aaisha's words were still echoing in my ear: "This too shall pass" but this goddamn night when I was stuck on the roof was not passing at all. It felt like years for me. "Divorce notice," I said in disgust. First, a feeling of anger overcame me, and then I was devastated. I decided to call Aaisha up and be truthful, whatever the result would be.

The next day, the operation head called my entire team and me for testimony. He looked very annoyed. I could feel the frustration in his words. He was sitting there with the national manager right in front of us, and I was standing there along with my entire team.

He emphasized each and every word to make sure that we were very clear about the outcome of that meeting. "Can you guys even imagine what kind of difficult phase we are passing through? I had to apologize to the entire board. It was very embarrassing. Now I have to personally vouch for the case to make sure that this is not a case of process lapses as it was presented. But the ultimate important question over here is of the data integrity, as emphasized by the auditor, and the company will not carry the burden of any person's arrogance. So please be truthful to me now. Have I made my point very clear?"

I knew that Sanchita had presented this case questioning the integrity of my boss as the data was sent from his mail id. Since he was heading the team, he was accountable. "Shantilal! I recall that you had already emphasized in our last review meet that at any given point of time, 5% of outstation cheques remain unreconciled and we had already presented it as an open risk, then why was such dubious data presented to auditors and who did that?"

"Sir, I can't answer who malfunctioned the data as I was on leave; however. I can show you the original file which clearly states the open item."

"Did anyone of you do that?" he asked, pointing to my team.

All of them shook their heads in the negative.

He glanced at the data saved on a share drive and stared at the national manager. "Isn't it apparent now?"

We left the room. After that incident, the whole team including me was very demoralised, de-motivated and devastated that despite all our efforts we were so humiliated and treated as culprits and of course, the entire team had to face the humiliation of non-performance, which was reflected in our half-yearly performance too.

Though nobody was sacked, over a period time my boss was kind of demoted. At one point of time, he was heading the entire team, but now he had been thrown into an isolated role, side-lined and thrown out of all the critical projects and meetings. Gradually, due to the humiliation, he left the job. A new manager was hired, who rejuvenated the whole team again and filled us with motivation and energy. As Aaisha had rightly said, "This too shall pass."

24

Rejuvenation

We both were faced with confrontation at that time. I was confronted with my new boss here, and she was confronted with her sister there. After that frustrating spell, I hardly had any trust left in the system. I was waiting for the right time to prove myself again.

At the team meeting when I put forward the idea of splitting the team, my new manager got furious with me. He asked everybody else to leave the meeting room except for me.

"Shants, I am doing this in your interest only," he said.

"By not trusting the team and its capability," I said.

"No! It's not like that. The organization is planning to change the entire system and process and considering your experience and your inputs in the previous project, I want you to take ownership of this project. None of them is a better fit than you. You are waiting for the right time, and this is your time, so grab this opportunity and prove yourself right."

I could not say anything more. I took whatever my boss had to offer me. We struggled for three months for days and nights to make it successful. Even when it was raining cats and dogs, and when the local trains, which are the lifeline of Mumbai, came to a halt, we reached office somehow. We continued to stay at the office until everything was back to normal. We feared that if we went out and got stuck, the entire month-end process would go for a toss, which was very critical from a business perspective as most of the booking of revenues happened in the last few days of the month.

Numerous people wanted us to fail. There was massive pressure from the business side. However my new boss, who had 12 years of experience in the political environment of one of the reputed banks, knew the nitty-gritty of dealing with people and he could very easily read between the lines and taught me too how to read the same, though still, I am not sure how much I have learned of it. I took the execution part of the process in my hand and kept focusing on it with my team while my boss dealt with people. We loved those three months of playing googlies, bouncers and pacers that came from various directions but finally, after three months, we came out successfully with flying colours.

My team had reached from dust to the sky in those three months. Once again, we were in the limelight. We made the project successful together. Finally, my manager informed me that we would be presenting to the board members about the project and the date scheduled for that meeting was the day just before Aaisha's birthday. Depending on the outcome of the meeting, further actions would be decided. Hence my manager asked me specifically not to absent myself for the entire week, meaning I could not meet her on her birthday.

At the same time, there she was struggling with her MBA exams and with her sister. As she did not have a personal mobile phone, I had to call her on her sister's mobile. She used this opportunity to tease both of us and blackmail her. She was so frustrated with her that she stopped talking to me when I called her on her sister's mobile. Then, either I had to call her on the landline number or had to wait until late at night when her father's mobile was available. Finally, she warned me that unless she had her own mobile phone, she wouldn't talk. In other words, that was another way of demanding that unless you gift me a mobile phone, there was a distant possibility of any further conversation. This is called a girl's way of demanding without blackmailing.

When we both were struggling those days, we never missed talking for a single day even though sometimes it was only for a few minutes. Now I wonder what we used to talk about at that time. I believe we spoke about the progress of my project, and she kept motivating me, or about my new manager, or about her MBA accounts questions at times. I helped her in understanding accounting concepts. After our marriage, when we both were living together, we hardly talked, and sometimes we wondered what to talk about. This is the beauty of the courtship period.

Anyway, her birthday was near. She solved my problem of selecting a gift, which was the most challenging task for me. Since I was swamped by my office project, reluctantly I had to tell her that I would not be able to come to Jaipur.

She was dejected on hearing this but knowing the urgency, she didn't say anything.

In those days, e-commerce was not available when you could order online. Unlike today, in those days, you needed friends who could help you. So I had to call my friend, Ashutosh, who had shifted to Jaipur and started his own practice. We discussed at length on the model to be gifted. Finally, we settled on a Sony Ericson Walkman phone- the best and the most expensive phone at that time, which cost me half of my month's salary. I would have never bought it for myself, but as rightly said when you are in love, money does not matter.

Ashutosh promised that he would deliver it the day before her birthday, and I would wish her happy birthday on her personal mobile. So without any further delay, he bought it for me, got it wrapped and headed towards her home to deliver it in person. At around 5 PM, he called me from her home, exactly half an hour before the most important meeting of my life and handed her the phone.

She wished me a good evening very coldly.

"Aren't you pleased with the gift?"

"Your friend is far better than you. At least he came and wished me in person."

"Oh! Don't forget that he came because of me only. Anyway, I wish you a very happy birthday in advance. I told you I have the most important meeting of my life and I have to go for that in another 15 minutes."

"Ah ok! Thanks and I loved the gift very much. I know you will do pretty well in the meeting and come out with flying colours. I very much wanted you to be here, by my side, on my birthday but I can understand your situation and considering the phase you have passed, career comes first but remember, not always."

"I do. Now I need to rush. Talk to you later." She rejuvenated me with confidence, and I approached the meeting room where my manager was already waiting outside for me with my national manager. At sharp 5.30 PM, the meeting started.

My operations head introduced me to the board members and mentioned me as the man behind this project's success. I made a brief presentation on the progress achieved and about future challenges and how we could overcome them. That was a proud moment for me when all the board members gave me a standing ovation. I looked towards my boss with tears of joy. I need not mention that this success was reflected in my annual appraisal too. I remembered Aaisha's words: "This too shall pass."

By the time the meeting got over, it was already 7 PM. When we came out, my boss congratulated me. I thanked him and told him that this would not have been possible without him. I asked him if I could take leave now and asked for one day's leave.

He said happily, "Enjoy your moment. Take leave now."

I approached Rajiv's desk knowing very well that except for him, all would have left for home by now. He was excited to know about my success. "It's time to celebrate but why do you look so dejected?"

I told him it was her birthday and I could not go to Jaipur. He quickly surfed the internet and told me that the next flight for Jaipur was scheduled at 10 PM. He did some quick calculations considering Mumbai traffic in his mind and said, "If you leave now, you will reach the airport max by 9.30 PM.." Without listening to my protests, he booked the ticket for the flight, took the printout and asked me to rush to the airport immediately.

"Don't you worry about your baggage? You tell us what you need on the phone and I will ask somebody to drop it at the airport from home."

I immediately started for the airport. Rajiv knew very well that only Kamal would have arrived home by that time. We all three coordinated on the phone and within half an hour, Kamal left from home along with my baggage. This time I didn't forget to ask him to bring along a bouquet of roses from Andheri station.

"Aha *ladka* Ayn Rand *se bahar nikal kar* romantic *ho gaya hai,*"(Aha the boy has come out of Ayn Rand's book and become romantic.) Kamal chuckled, and we all three laughed on the phone.

We both reached the airport at 9 PM. I boarded the aircraft, and I was on my way to Jaipur. At 11.30 PM, I reached Jaipur airport and took a cab for her home, which was just 15 minutes away from the airport. At sharp midnight, I called her from outside her house, "Wish you a very happy birthday, my darling."

"Thank you. I knew that you will be the first one to wish me; however, I would be pleased if you were here with me at this moment."

"Oh! I am sorry darling but if you really want, I can fulfil this dream of yours right now."

"You are a God or some kind of Jinn who will appear by the snap of your finger?"

"You just close your eyes and wish."

"I wish…"

"Okay open the gate now…I will appear."

"What? Don't crack any jokes else I will kill you."

"*Arre!* Seriously, open the gate. It's cold outside."

She sneaked out and was amazed to see me outside with the bouquet in my hand. She could not believe her eyes and rubbed them a thousand times. She quietly came out, and I just hugged her tightly.

That day we celebrated her birthday along with her family. In the evening, I took my flight back to Mumbai. That day cost me my entire month's salary including the gift but the price paid was nothing against the memories I cherished. Even today, I hear her words, "Before marriage, darling, anything and after marriage, darling, let me sleep and don't disturb me".

25

That Terrifying
but Heavenly Day

It was time to jump ship, and along with my boss, I joined one of the most reputed banks in the world. Before joining, I was asked to produce my membership number, which I had not obtained. So in a way it was good for me as my boss agreed to delay my joining by a month on the condition that I would not be granted leave for more than a week at the time of my marriage, which was just three months away. Of course, I chose Jaipur to finish off my management training classes for getting CA membership, which was a mandatory prerequisite for the job.

Once again, I landed in Jaipur and stayed with my cousin who was doing engineering. His college was in Malviya Nagar. He was staying just four houses away from her home. That was the most convenient option and benefited me in two ways – I need not worry about a vehicle as I got his bike and I was staying next to her, so it was very convenient for us to meet. Though it might have been awkward for her family and her neighbours that the would-be son-in-law was staying just next to them, we were sitting on the peak of the Everest of love, so who gave a shit about people? I didn't care much.

By that time, she too had completed her MBA and had joined the retail banking branch of another reputed bank in India. Those fifteen days just flew like seconds. Till now, we believe that was the best time of our life. It was the month of sweet November.

Our daily schedule was fixed. In the morning I had to go to classes, and she had to go to the office. At 4.30 PM, before bank closing time for customers, I would reach her office. Initially, her manager was sceptical of me but after she introduced me to him, I could hear the comments of her colleagues with a lot of chuckles, "Aaisha! Time to go." Since she was one of the youngest in her office, her manager, who knew her father, let her go early.

I picked her up from the office and together we would explore places in the pink city. There was not a single place left be it restaurants, tea/coffee joints, pubs or discos, which had been left unvisited be it Angara disco where we danced endlessly all alone on the dance floor or Tapri in front of Central Park or the famous Juice Centre in C-Scheme or the well-known Murli Panwala at Ajmeri Gate.

But our all-time favourite destination was Jawahar Circle, where we would stay until dusk. By that time, people would start leaving. We were left alone in one of the corner seats. The cold winter days made the weather more romantic, and we sat very close, holding hands. My fingers would caress her but she knew exactly when and where to stop me. Those were times of beautiful moonlight and her face would glitter like a diamond in the moonlight. In those moments, I cradled, cuddled and hugged her tightly and kissed her all over.

My cousin's place in Jawahar Nagar was another place where we used to meet, where we had all the privacy a new couple needed as both my cousin and her husband went to work. The entire home was left open for us.

Once I took her over there. We were alone. She was wearing a white shirt and denim jeans. We were comfortably sitting on the couch. She laid down her head in my lap, and I was combing her hair with my fingers. I didn't know whether it was a boon or a curse that whenever she found herself in a comfortable situation, she immediately fell asleep. Her eyes were closed. Her face was very calm and cute, like an innocent child.

I suddenly felt a burning desire in my heart. I bent down and put my lips on my love. I grabbed her face firmly in my palms so that I could kiss her on her lips. I knew she was not sleeping, but this is the beauty of girls - when they don't want to resist, they act innocent. However, they are well aware of their limits. Probably this time, she had extended my boundaries or perhaps she was experimenting, giving me a free hand to see up to what limit I would go.

We kissed passionately for a long time. We started enjoying those moments. We were lost entirely within. From lips to tongue to saliva, everything was becoming one. I didn't realize when my hand had unbuttoned the top two buttons of her shirt, and my hand slipped inside. I could feel the softness which was nothing less than soft velvet like a Kashmiri Pashmina which is warm by nature. I felt like I was standing on top of a hill and nourishing those heavenly moments for my lifetime.

I was burning with desire. I slowly rested her head on the couch. I moved on top of her and was kissing and sucking her madly. Now I became naughtier but before I could unzip her jeans, she pushed me so hard that I fell down from the couch to the floor and my head struck the centre table. I was in pain.

Now she was wide awake and standing upright in front of me. She commented, "Boys will always be boys and always have the same target for girls. Keep something for after marriage." She buttoned her top and went outside, on to the balcony.

I could not make anything from her flat, expressionless face. I didn't know whether she was angry or annoyed. She was not smiling. I followed her to the balcony, and for a long time, we did not utter a single word. I could not as I was filled with guilt and embarrassment due to my lousy behaviour and she could not because she did not want to talk about it anymore.

To make the atmosphere lighter, I asked her, "Do you want to have *masala* tea? I can make it for you."

"Not interested and let's go now," she snapped.

That day we did not talk anymore. I didn't know then that more terrifying days still lay ahead.

26

Finally We
Were Happily Married

Though I could not forget any of those days, that particular day shattered and scared both of us. That was the day we went to Clarks Amer for dinner – one of the best places near her home in the pink city. It was a rooftop restaurant on the sixth floor and had a bar. We have gone for a candlelight dinner. Except for a few foreigners and a few guests, the restaurant was almost empty. We were enjoying our candlelit moments when suddenly, out of nowhere, four heavily built men appeared and settled themselves at the bar counter. Two of them were bearded. They looked like local goons. Though they never came near us or tried to provoke us, they were staring at us, which made her very conscious. I advised her not to pay any attention and told her she need not worry about them. I told her to try and enjoy the dinner; however, my advice would not calm her. She insisted on leaving the place as soon as possible.

We quickly finished our dinner and left the restaurant. Outside was a beautiful, attractive antique gallery where I asked her to take a few snaps. We were alone there. Those were not the days of selfies, and mobile phones did not have a front camera, so we were taking snaps one by one. Suddenly the four men appeared in the gallery. One of them came to me and said, grinning, "Let me take a snap of both of you." The three men behind laughed loudly.

Our hearts started pounding very fast, but I tried to maintain my composure and analysed the situation, looking for an option if something went wrong. For sure, I would not be able to take a single one of them down owing to my physique. Still, I did a quick calculation in my mind. If the situation warranted, I thought of the option of grabbing hold of one of the metal antiques and hitting them with it, which might give us a small window for running.

He once again insisted, "What are you thinking? Let me take a snap of both you together." She was scared to death and came and stood behind me. I tried to calm her and thought I would let him take a pic so that we wouldn't provoke them by saying no, though she said from behind, "Thanks! That is not required. We are leaving now."

Then one of three guys said, sniggering, "Hey don't frighten them. Let them enjoy in their own way." He stepped back, and all of us approached the lift. When the lift arrived once again, they requested, "There is enough space over here, you may join us." But I said smiling, "No that's fine". We will leave in some time."

"But you said you were leaving now," and they started laughing loudly.

The doors of the lift closed; however, we could still hear their guffaws. We waited for some time. She suggested we use the stairs. We didn't know if they would be waiting for us downstairs. We slowly climbed down. When we reached the hotel lobby, I could not see any sign of them; however, she was still frightened. I tried to calm her. She did not believe me and said, "You know they were drunk."

"So what? Even we drink sometimes. Drinking does not mean that you are a goon."

"But they looked like goons."

"Sometimes, looks can be deceptive, and it does not mean they are hoodlums. We should not be judgmental."

"Whatever. God has given the gift of instinct to girls. I can smell danger."

Anyway, we waited for some more time in the lobby and then left for home. It was 9 PM. By Jaipur standards, we were late, and I knew her father would be angry if we didn't leave for home immediately.

But then she asked me a burning question, which disturbed me, "What if something had gone wrong? What would have you done to save me?"

For a while I remained speechless but then I said earnestly, "That is true I am not a He-Man or Superman or a filmy hero who can handle ten villains together. I may not be able to take one of them down, but one thing is for sure I would have fought until my last breath irrespective of what was the result. I would not have allowed any of them to touch you. But even if something had gone wrong,

I would not have left you alone. I will always stand by your side come what may."

She did not speak a single word, and we left for home. Time flew. When fifteen days were over, I didn't realize it. I reached Mumbai and got busy with my new office. We both were excited to start our new life together. We talked for hours and hours on the phone as every couple talk, and even while talking, we got sexually excited.

I remember we had a small fight over our honeymoon too. I didn't want to go immediately after marriage as I was going to get only a week's leave as promised by my boss. I wanted to go later when I would get fifteen days off. But as usual, she prevailed. Finally, we agreed on a short trip of three days to Kulu-Manali, in the lap of the Himalayas.

Finally, the fateful day of our wedding arrived. With all the usual events and traditions, we were happily married. We were now, as rightly said in India, '*do jism, ek jaan*' for the rest of our seven life terms. In Indian mythology, this way of life is called *Ardhnariswarroop*. Now all my secrets belonged to her, and all aspects of her life belonged to me. I had already made arrangements to start our new life in Mumbai. Our married life began to take off.

From the canteen to lunch box, from Babloo's boring *parathas* to a variety of breakfasts and delicious dinners – she took control of every nook and cranny of my life. I did not have to worry about anything. Those were the days when we would roam around Nariman Point for endless hours during the weekends. From enjoying the rain together to celebrating every festival – everything had changed, and with that change, when one year had passed, we did not even realize it. In the meanwhile, she joined the Mumbai Andheri branch of her bank. The Mayavi Nagri took control of our lives and started driving it tediously but that was not the end of the story; it was the fresh start of another struggle. Life moved on, and along with that we both moved on and took the plunge into our new life.

We wanted to control any further changes but life had already designed its own path, and everything changed on that terrible night of 26/11.

Part III

27

Our Family Flourished

The night when I was stuck on the cot, seemed much longer than I could believe. The same way when it was too long on 26/11. The clock showed 11.30 PM. There was no sign of her. Keeping aside everything, I decided to call her. I dialled her number several times but she did not respond, the same way I did not react on that night of 26/11, and for the first time in my life, I realized the frustration of what it feels like when somebody hangs up on you.

The memory of the 26/11 night is still fresh in my mind; it was a night that terrified not just us but all of India, where the tragic war continued for three days. We were all glued to our television sets. We didn't dare to move outside our home. You never knew what would happen next and how many terrorists were spread across the city. When the government announced that the terrorists were confined to a specific area and that the situation was under control, we breathed a deep sigh of relief.

On that fateful evening of 26/11, our whole team decided to go out for a movie, for the 9 PM show. My office was in Andheri, and there was a PVR Multiplex nearby. Though I had informed her of the evening plan, as usual, my phone was out of charge. While we were enjoying the movie, my boss got a message about gunfire in the city. First, we thought it might be a gang war between two underworld groups, which is very common in Mumbai; however, in those fights, the common public was never injured. By the time we came out of the cinema at midnight, everybody's mobile had started popping up with messages and calls. It was then that we realized that the situation was much worse than we thought. Anyway, we decided to leave and to call everyone to ensure that everybody reached home safely.

I started off on my bike, and found that the whole city was converted into a war zone; the police were guarding every nook and corner of the town like a fort. When I reached Andheri Bridge to get on to the Western Express highway, I was stopped by the police. They told me that the road ahead was blocked as some 700m ahead, to the left of the bridge towards Bandra, a bomb had exploded in a taxi just half an hour ago. I was horrified to hear the news. The explosion had claimed three lives including the driver of the car, and the car was blown to pieces. I told them I needed to go right towards Borivali. The police thoroughly checked me. I told them I was returning from office. As I had to turn right, they allowed me to go.

I was scared and sweating but a little comforted by the police who were guarding every corner. I was still unaware of what was happening in the city. Shocked and shaking with fear, I reached home and rang the doorbell; she opened the door. As soon as she saw me, she hugged me tightly. She was crying profusely. Her eyes were puffed and reddish, and she snarled, "Where the hell were you? What happened to your phone? We've been trying desperately for the last one hour. Don't you know what is happening in the city?"

I definitely knew something was wrong but till then, I didn't exactly know what was happening in the city. "We are being attacked by thousands of terrorists and thousands of people are already killed," she said

"What?" I exclaimed and looked at the television immediately. Every news channel was giving updates every second. Meanwhile, I got calls from both the homes (mine and my in-laws' as they too had been trying to reach me) to ask about my well-being. I assured them we were all right and safe.

The whole night, we were glued to the TV and didn't even blink our eyes. I didn't even realize when she fell asleep in my lap on the sofa. Many top police officers were already martyred and, in the morning, the situation was not good. In fact, it was turning worse but at least now, the armed forces were in action so the terrorists were confined to some places only. That day was announced as a holiday in Mumbai keeping security in mind, and only critical staff was summoned to work. Thankfully I was not on that list. By evening, the situation was better and under control. Thanks to the armed forces.

But that day, another unexpected change was also waiting for me for which I was not even ready. It was another round of bombs falling on me. In the evening she told me that she was not feeling well and felt like vomiting and that her periods were delayed. We immediately went to a nearby doctor. After an initial check-up, she asked us to do a pregnancy check first thing in the morning to ensure it was not related to pregnancy. We bought the kit and waited eagerly for the morning.

We read all the instructions carefully and did the test at home first thing in the morning. Initially, only one line appeared. We were relieved that it was negative.. But after a while, the second line appeared, and we were stunned. My first reaction was, "How the hell is this possible despite all the protection?" I was not even sure whether I should be dancing with amazement or crying in sorrow. One thing for sure, I didn't want it to happen now as I thought we were not ready since we were struggling in our careers.

But, with all the impossible things that were happening in the world, why couldn't this happen? We both discussed the possibilities; however she firmly ruled out all of them except for the fact we were going to accept the reality and she said firmly, "This too shall pass."

We reached out to a gynaecologist and when she showed us a view of our new life on the ultrasound monitor, all my doubts drifted away. I was just gazing at her in excitement and my eyes were wet. I tried to hide them from her and the doctor, but both noticed and smiled back. "Yes you are now going to be a father. How is the feeling?" said the doctor.

"I can't describe it. Earlier I was full of doubts. Now I am as determined as a mountain," I replied.

"The baby is now one and a half months old. It will be due somewhere in July." She gave us all the necessary instructions and from that day onwards, our world changed. We were eagerly waiting for this new life. I preferred a baby girl, but she did not seem to have any preference.

Both the families wholeheartedly celebrated her *Aathva* (a celebration at eight months). Post that, she stayed back with my parents in Bharatpur. I returned to Mumbai and finally, the fateful day had come when she was taken to the hospital at night. I booked the next available flight to Jaipur, as it is the nearest airport from Bharatpur, which was the next morning. I eagerly waited up the whole night. Every hour, I kept calling to know the status. Finally, when I was about to leave for Jaipur in the morning, I got a call from my father, *"Beta tu baap ban gaya. Ladka hua hai."* (You have become father. It's a baby boy.)

I cannot describe in words what I felt at that moment but one thing for sure, I was dying to see both of them. When I reached my hometown, instead of going home first, I rushed to the hospital. By then, both of them were shifted to the room. I was so excited to see them that while I was opening the door to the room, my hands were trembling.

As soon as I entered the room, our eyes met and, understanding my curiosity, she signalled towards him. He was lying beside her. He was so cute, so delicate, like some antique, so reddish, like the sun that had just risen from the east, and his skin was like the fur of a rabbit. I held him very carefully. I cannot tell in words what a father feels like when he first holds his child in his hands. We named him Shreyansh, inspired by Shreayanshnath, who is one of the *Teerthankars* (Gods) in the Jain community.

Time started flying as we settled into our new life. Now she was a mother and this is the most valued relationship in any girl's life. Everything else was left behind. Her child became her utmost priority.

We did not want to put him in day care and my parents were reluctant to shift to Mumbai. At the same time, my bank was setting up a new back office in Jaipur. So multiple opportunities were arising over there. Since Jaipur was like my other hometown too, my parents would happily agree to shift to Jaipur instead of Mumbai. So considering all the odds in my favour, I grabbed the opportunity in Jaipur and moved there. She also got a transfer very quickly.

Shifting to Jaipur, for me, was like a new chapter of my life and at that time, I didn't know what a significant change it was going to bring in my life. From a fast-paced monotonous and mechanical life to a slow-paced, enriching and luxurious growth (not in terms of money but in terms of time as now you could afford to have a home and car too, something you couldn't even dream of in Mumbai. Even though you can afford a car in Mumbai, you can't drive it primarily due to parking issues and secondly due to traffic, which made your life nothing less than hell) and with an entirely different work culture and environment. Initially, I found it challenging to cope but as time passed, I learned many other aspects of life and only God knows what more I was going to see in the future very soon. But all these changes applied to me alone and her life was the same as usual. With the added load of being a mother, she was far busier. In that seesaw of life, we never even realized how another year had passed.

28

Employee of the Year

In Jaipur, the finance process was just setting up after being carved out from a business management division and hence it had its own challenges. I always love to work in a challenging environment as when you succeed in that, it gives you a sense of accomplishment. It feels like life is worthy. Of course, we work for money. However, it cannot be a complete source of motivation at work. You feel more motivated when your efforts are acknowledged and rewarded. Without that, it will be a lifeless mechanical job. It becomes more critical when you are spending half of your waking hours in the office.

Though it was the enhanced back office unit of the bank, the environment was more like KPOs/BPOs and outside the office, people always thought that we were working in call centres as we supported UK hours, went to the office at odd hours and cabs were deployed to pick and drop us. Whenever we try to explain to people that it was not a call centre but an enhanced unit of the bank only, their next question would be, "Okay, where is the branch?" since they thought of a traditional bank and knew nothing about investment banking. So in the end, we gave up explaining and merely nodded our heads in agreement.

The most significant change for me was the environment, dealing with local banking clients/customers with a robust, regulated and demanding timeline. There was a month-end process to meet. Mostly the team consisted of senior stakeholders, local clients and colleagues, the tone always had to be professional and it was hardly fun. You were utterly bogged down in the files. But here the environment was completely different. Though we had global stakeholders and here too we had deadlines to meet, the people were comparatively more casual. It may be because of a younger, highly motivated workforce. Having fun at work was part of the official agenda and an objective of management. Here we had dedicated committees to promote building a great workplace together unlike in front office. Here, having lunch or tea breaks were official, and our stakeholders expected and understood it very well, unlike in front office where longer breaks of more than ten minutes filled us with guilt. Here we had the concept of hard and lighter days too, where hard days meant you had to stay in office as long as 12 to 15 hours and meet the deadline and easy days were the ones where you were expected to invest in yourself, learning and developing yourself.

Anyway, I quickly adapted to the environment. I started enjoying it; however, Aaisha became more stressed and she was struggling. She woke up early in the morning, got the household chores done and by the time I woke up, she was ready to leave for office. She prepared breakfast and kept it on the dining table. When my parents were travelling, she made my lunch too. When I walked her to her bike, she would peck me on my cheeks, say goodbye to me and take leave. Effectively, that was the only private time we had to communicate with each other in a loving manner.

When my parents were not there, I would drop Shreyansh at my in-law's place. Then I left for office as per my UK time at 11.30 AM. The whole day she grappled with demanding customers in the bank and managed to achieve her targets and finally in the evening, when she came home by 7 PM, she was thoroughly exhausted. By the time I came back home, she was already in bed snoring. She had to work six days a week. Since we were living in Jaipur and near our in-law's place, our Sundays were almost always spent in my in-law's home. So in a nutshell, our private life was quite screwed; however, we did not realize it at that time as we both were too busy to bother with that and time was passing smoothly.

The annual event of my office was held at the Marriot. It was a grand event where even families were invited with a splendid stage, choreographed events including dances, music and fashion shows, and above all, delicious food. At this event, the efforts of the top talents were acknowledged and employees of the year were awarded at the site level.

I attended the event along with her. She was standing by my side and enjoying herself. After the official inauguration of the program, the first event was the price distribution. When the employee of the year was announced, the crowd started cheering. At that moment she asked me, "Shants! When are you going to get this prestigious award?

"You have demanded it just now. Next year you will find me on that stage." I grinned, and she chuckled and said, "As if your management is waiting for me to tell them." She guffawed so loudly that people nearby could hear her.

I caught her hand, placed it near my heart and said a very filmy dialogue, "*Agar kisi cheez ko tum dil se chaho to sari qaynat tumhe us se milane ki sajish rachne lagta hai.* (If you want something wholeheartedly, the whole world will conspire to make you meet with it). You will see, next time I will be standing on that stage." Once again, she convulsed with laughter but this time in a controlled manner and just said, "Yes you will."

Those three words, "Yes you will," sounded as if they had been uttered by Ma Saraswati and at that time I was not sure if the next year was going to be a reality.

29
Mishika

Our department was involved in setting up an activity-based costing process for the investment banking division. Our finance department was located in two places. A majority of the team was in Mumbai, and a small unit of 10 people was situated in Jaipur. Since the department was expanding, it was decided to hire new, qualified accountant talent. Though most of the hiring was happening in Mumbai, it was decided to hire one person in Jaipur for smooth transitioning. Since in my team it was all men, it was decided to employ a diversity candidate. The candidate was finalized, and Mishika was hired. She was supposed to join us within two weeks. Everybody in the team was excited. Finally, our team too would have some diversity.

On the day she joined, all the boys were fighting like kids to receive her from reception. Finally, it was Deependra who went to receive her after a lot of hustle and bustle. Her parents came to drop her on her first day to the office. Deependra brought her to my desk. She was of average height with wheatish complexion and sharp features.

Her hair was below shoulder length and tied back with a band. She had a wide smile and was extremely charming.

Deependra introduced us. We smiled at each other, shook hands and I welcomed her aboard. Though her name was Mishika, I always called her Mishh. Since she was the youngest and a fresher, she was given additional responsibility for all the team building activity. She tried to revive the team by all means. From celebrating birthdays to arranging parties (though she never went to any of party for two reasons. One she was the only girl in the team, and she could not afford to be partnered with drinkers. Two, mainly because of her family who was a bit conservative.) Everything was handled by her earnestly, soberly and eagerly and we all got engrossed in the events though initially, I was very indifferent to her. I never thought that I was going to be the one who would hook her until the last minute.

It was her birthday. She was expecting that we would arrange something for her. As usual, boys are shamelessly indifferent and ungrateful. We didn't do anything. We never even bothered to get her a cake as a gesture of gratitude for whatever efforts she had put in to revive the place. She became very agitated. Finally, to make her happy, we decided to throw a party for her, but the biggest challenge was to get approval from her father. I took the responsibility, and she reluctantly gave me her father's number, knowing that he would never approve.

I called him, introduced myself and tried to convince him. When she always did so much for us, I requested him to let her go for a dinner party subject to certain conditions that it would be simple vegetarian dinner without drinks, near her home, would not be later than 10 PM and that we would drop her home safely.

I put on a sad face, and by seeing the expression on my face, she cried, "I knew my father would never agree. In fact, now he will scold me at home asking why I even allowed you to call him in the first place, knowing that he doesn't like me going out alone with boys."

"Yeah! You are right. He was not only sceptical but also insecure."

"Don't say anything about my father."

"But he is…"

"I said please don't say anything. I know he is a bit obsessed with me because I am the only daughter and he does not trust anybody easily, but it does not mean he is not a good father."

"Okay, as you say, but now can you please tell us some good place near your home where we can celebrate your birthday."

"It means he allowed. It is impossible."

"Of course he did."

"You are the only one who has been able to convince my father. He never allowed me to go out even with my relatives. I don't know how you did it but still I am suspicious that something is not right."

"Now don't bother about it. Your father gave exclusive permission but of course with certain conditions."

Anyway, we celebrated her birthday. Since the place was next to her house, instead of us dropping her, her father himself came to pick her up, possibly to check whether we had fulfilled our promises or not. She introduced each one of us to him. From his expression, I could see that he was quite furious; however, he did not say anything in front of us; he just smirked.

Next day I asked her why her father had been so furious. He was angry that she did not tell him that she was the only girl at the party. He worried that if somebody had seen her with so many boys, people would have formed an opinion that she partied with boys.

"Oh God! What a conservative man he is!" I said, irritated.

"Don't say anything about my father. Whatever way he is, I love him." And the discussion ended.

Everything was going smooth, and life was moving as usual. Meanwhile, my darling Aaisha and I were growing distant from each other slowly and gradually, because of our timing issues; we did not even realize what was happening to us. We were just living under the same roof but hardly talking to each other.

After a few months, one fine day, our top management visited Jaipur. We were all called to the meeting room. Though the news was airing on the floor that our process might be consolidated in Mumbai, every time I tried to confirm it with my manager, he always refuted it. Since that day I was sceptical and now the day had come when it was announced that to bring in efficiencies, the process was going to be consolidated in Mumbai. "But it does not mean that you will be asked to leave. Either you decide to join us in Mumbai, and you will be compensated and rewarded for that or we will help you in searching for new roles in Jaipur. Until you are settled down in your new processes, we will not bind the finance division. Till then you will continue to work from Jaipur." Our management tried to console and assure us. What other option were we left with except for accepting what they had to offer?

A few of us decided to quit the bank, a few shifted to Mumbai, taking the compensation and reward and finally only two of us, Mishika, and I, were left who had to search for new roles. Since I had shifted from Mumbai due to personal reasons, I did not want to move back to Mumbai and she, of course, could not move as her parents would never allow her to live alone in Mumbai. She was a gold medallist, ranked in CA, and had so many wonderful opportunities in her hand but due to her parents, she had to let go of them. So how could she even think of accepting such an offer? Our decisions were respected, and new roles were being looked at for us, which would best fit our expectations.

So for all practical purposes, we had a job, but we did not have any work to do as all the work was transited to Mumbai over time. The whole day, we looked at each other's faces, spending time on Google, having longer breaks than usual and there was nobody to stop us.

30

Once Again
My Love Reappeared

In Jaipur, our office was situated outside the city. The campus was huge. Our schedule was fixed. We logged in to the office at 12.30 PM, went for a one-hour tea break, came back to the desk, did some work, googled news or other areas of interest, went for lunch again at around 3 PM for an hour. At approximately 5 PM, again we went for a long one-hour tea break and roamed around campus and finally at 8.30 PM, we left for home. We were becoming closer.

But it was also true that I was getting obsessed with her. It became very difficult for me to pass the time in office without her. When she was on leave, I called her at least five times to remind her how bored I was feeling. It became next to impossible for me to spend time in office without her. When she was not in the office, I just kept a close watch on the time and wondered if there were more than 24 hours in a day.

However, over the last few days I observed that her behaviour had changed and she seemed to be agitated.

Whenever I tried to push her for a break, she became frustrated, which was not the case earlier. At times, I kept pinging her on Messenger and she did not even reply. She seemed lost in her own world. The more I tried to push her to talk, the more infuriated she became.

She abruptly stopped going for lunch and tea breaks with me and whenever I asked her, she made some lame excuses, which I didn't believe. I observed she was trying to avoid me. When it became completely unbearable for me, I slid my chair next to her and asked, "What happened to you? Why are you behaving like this? What have I done wrong? Unless you tell me, how will I know?"

"What has happened to me?" she replied coldly, without even looking at me.

"Don't you know what has happened? I mean you have stopped talking to me completely and you're trying to avoid me," I urged.

"Shants! That's my wish? It's only me who will decide to whom I choose to talk and take a break or go for lunch with. That's none of your business. Do you understand that?" she replied, annoyed.

I was bewildered by her answer but still I was not ready to give up on her. I pushed her further and put my hand on her shoulder and said comfortingly, "Is there something which is bothering you? Please tell me. I am your friend. Am I not?"

She shrugged my hands from her shoulder and said angrily, "Meet me outside right now," and she walked away coldly.

I dragged my feet to go outside, wondering what wrong I had done. She was standing in a corner staring out of the glass window. When I reached there, she turned towards me. I could see her face was red with anger. She blurted, "Shants! This is office and I don't want to create any scene on the floor. You dare touch me again. I am not your girlfriend or slave who will always follow you and go for lunch or tea breaks according to your wish. Next time, if you bother me again, that will not be good for you so mind your own business and leave me alone." And she walked away.

I was stunned to hear her words. But this time I was angry and thrown off balance by what had just happened. From that day onwards, I stopped bothering her but I was disturbed by what had happened. I was wondering how she could even think that I was falling for her. I was wondering what wrong I had done to her that she was forced to think that way. I was traumatized and stressed by the incident and even Aaisha could sense the change in my behaviour. She even asked me but I just ignored her and excused myself, saying that it was just due to office pressure.

Our homes fell on the same route and we were usually allotted the same cab on the way to office or home. Earlier Mishika would fight with other colleagues from different departments to sit with me but now she sat quietly away from me. It was just not me but even the other colleagues who noticed the difference in her behaviour. She seemed to be distressed and I could clearly see the pain in her eyes but she didn't want to share it with anybody.

Several days passed and I was trying to adjust without her in office though still wondering what had gone wrong.

One day in the middle of the night when I was sleeping, my mobile buzzed. Since I was not a sound sleeper, I woke up. It was a message from Mishika, "Shants! I am really sorry for my behaviour. I know I should not talk to you that way."

I was shocked to see her message. It was 1 AM. I wondered whether I should reply or not. Against my wish I replied, "Now what happened?"

"Nothing. Just wanted to apologize to you," she replied.

"You can say that in the office too." I replied.

"Yeah but I feel like talking to you now. Can we talk now?"

"What do you think? I am a buffoon or what with whom you can behave whatever way you like?" I messaged her.

"I am really sorry☒" My phone buzzed again.

With the continuous beeps of messages, Aaisha turned sideways. In order to not disturb her, I went outside the bedroom. Meanwhile, a message flashed again, "Can we talk now?"

"Can't it wait until morning? What about your parents? Will not they mind that their daughter is talking to a stranger in the middle of the night?" I replied.

After that there was a long pause. Initially I was reluctant to talk at that weird hour but considering the timing of her message, I knew she was in distress. After a long time, she wanted to share her story so I didn't want to discourage her. Additionally, I was curious to know the reason for this sudden change. So I messaged her, "Okay call me now."

Since my parents too were sleeping in the room next to the drawing room and considering the volume of my voice, , I went upstairs in order to not disturb anyone. It was the month of September so the nights were becoming colder outside due to the heavy monsoon rains that year and therefore, to protect myself, I wrapped myself in Aaisha's shawl.

Mishika called me. Her voice sounded low and distressed.

"Shants! I am really sorry for what happened. I did not mean to hurt you but I couldn't help it. You can't even imagine what I have gone through." While saying this, she started crying.

I did not speak for a long time and I let her cry so that she could feel lighter after the storm of tears in her eyes passed. After a while, she said, "Shants! You there?"

"Yeah. I am here. I understand that you were going through a terrible time. There must be some distressing story behind your behaviour. So are you comfortable to share what really happened? If you don't feel like sharing it then I don't want to push you but I want my Mishh the way she was. Charming and energetic. This sombre behaviour does not suit you well."

"I will try to but I am not sure whether I will ever feel the way I was earlier."

"You definitely will. Now tell me what happened and I will try to help you in whatever way I can."

"There is this guy named Vivek whom I loved so much. He lived in the corner house in the same row as mine. We were friends since our childhood. We went to the same school and grew up together. We loved each other so much that we couldn't even imagine living without each other. He is still pursuing his engineering from IIT Delhi. He might take another two to three years to settle down. Since I am already a Chartered Accountant and working, my father wants me to get married as soon as possible."

"So what is the issue? Why don't you tell your father about it? He might wait for a year or two. Won't he?" I said cutting her midway.

"Shants! Will you hear me out please?"

"Aah okay. Tell me."

"I talked to Vivek and told him about my situation, about how my parents were pressurizing me to get married as soon as possible. He told me that he would talk to his family once he was back in Jaipur. Last week he was in Jaipur and we both decided to communicate to our parents simultaneously. I told my parents. They were very angry but after initial resistance and since I am their only daughter and considering my happiness, they agreed to talk to his parents. They asked me to call him at home. I called him but he told me that he could not come as he couldn't dare to face either his parents or mine. He didn't inform his parents about us. I was broken and very angry at his cowardly behaviour. But my father didn't want to give up so easily on his only daughter's dreams so my parents visited his place.

"His parents insulted my parents like anything. They even mentioned that I trapped their intelligent and innocent son and that my parents encouraged me to trap an IIT-ian so that they could get a bright son-in-law without spending a single penny. My father became very furious and they insulted them back. He said that my daughter is my pride, so don't even dare to utter a single word against her. Before my father got into a fight with them, my mother dragged him out. They were very disappointed in me. Initially I could not believe what had just happened but I was more aggrieved at Vivek's behaviour. He was a mere bystander when his parents were insulting mine.

"My parents were very dejected. I apologized and they easily forgave me. I promised them I would not let them feel down again in my life. I immediately broke up with him and vowed not to talk to him again in my life. He kept calling me for a few days but when I warned him that the next time he called me again I would go to police, he stopped calling me. He kept on sending messages asking me to listen to his part of story but I ignored him completely."

"You did the right thing. If I had been in your place, I would have thrashed him like anything," I said consoling her.

"I know that I am right but since he was my first love, I was not able to forget him. I don't know why my heart said I should listen to him once," she said.

"I don't think you should ever talk to him again in your life. Better to forget him. You don't deserve such a spineless guy. You will find a much better guy in this world. I know it's difficult to forget your first love but you have to be brave," I said.

"Are you sure I will find a much better guy than him?" She was sceptical about it.

"Of course you will. I bet. You are such a beautiful, charming and intelligent girl; who will say no to you? If I would have been in that fool's place, I would not have let such a chance go like this. He was an idiot. Tell me what kind of guy you want. I will search for one for you," I assured her.

"Okay! So would you have married me if you were in his place?" she asked.

"Of course. You bet." I said.

"Don't tell me you are falling for me?" she said jokingly.

"Earlier I thought I was falling for you but now I am sure I am in love with you." I smirked.

"Shants! There is no chance for you. You are already married and old," she said, laughing now.

"So what? Love knows no boundaries," I said laughing.

"...and don't forget you have a son too?" she said.

"So what? Abroad, that's very common," I said sniggering.

"But we are in India so you don't have a chance. Stop flirting with me and start looking for a guy for me who is exactly like you," she said

"Wow! I can't even flirt with you but you need a guy like me," I said sarcastically.

"Shants! Bye. Goodnight," she said, ignoring me.

"Ah okay. Forget it but tell me one thing. Will you be the same Mishh from today onwards like before? I can't bear this irritating girl anymore, and promise me that going forward you will not hide anything from me. Whenever you feel bothered, you will talk to me and I will try to resolve all your problems as much as I can," I said.

"I will and thank you very much for being there for me. I can't thank you anymore," she said.

"Goodnight and have sweet dreams of your new prince from now on and forget that bastard. Okay? And see you tomorrow in office," I said.

"Goodnight." And she cut the call.

I came downstairs and slipped into the bed assuming that Aaisha was still in deep sleep and dreaming, but actually that was not the case. However, she didn't say anything to me at that time.

From that day onwards, Mishika tried to behave, as usual as she was but she was still not the same. I know with passing time every wound will be healed but when the wounds are like this, it is going to take a much longer time.

From that day on, her father started searching for a groom for her. Not to mention he became more conservative from that day on. After all, his trust and pride had been smashed like a glass and that wound definitely would not heal until he found a better groom for her.

From that day, she shared everything with me including how her parents were looking for a boy for her, how her dates went with prospective grooms and how her father had rejected all the guys due to one or other reason or about how things could not be settled because of dowry agreements. She became depressed when she liked a boy, but he did not like her. She took that as a rejection and then I had to comfort her. She said, "I wish I could have a love story like yours."

I just smiled in return and thought, "Yes Aaisha and I had a wonderful love story; however nowadays it seems lost somewhere as she doesn't have any time for me." It's not that she did not want to spend time with me, but it was because of our different office timings, her sincerity towards her job, motherhood and of course, hardly any privacy left due to the joint family. If she had time to spare, she had to spend it at her parent's place. Barely any romance was left in our life. It may be because of boredom or tight schedules, but all the excitement was gone from our lives. The only excitement that was left in our lives was our son but we had different views about him too. I felt we need not worry about him as he would find his own path like we did but her point of view was very different, and she wanted to control every aspect of his life

One fine day, Mishika and I were roaming around after evening tea. Though it was the month of September, it was a hot and humid that day. Anyway, the cool air was comforting. That day I was a bit dejected, and Mishh asked, "What happened, Shants?"

"Nothing, just thinking. This whole year will be wasted just because of this stupid transition. What do you think, how will our performance be rated without work?"

"But it's not our fault, right?" She smirked.

"But still, we will be penalized for no fault of ours. This is how the corporate world works. Since we are leavers, our existing department will not take care of us or might be, my promotion will be screwed and in the new department, we will have to prove ourselves again and all the work done till now will go down the drain," I replied in an irritated tone.

She fell silent for a while.

"Shants! Tell me one thing. Imagine if your life could be reversed, and you could go back to your childhood days, how different will you make it from now?"

"What kind of question is this? I am not sure," I shrugged.

"Just imagine. If you were not a CA and not working in a bank, what would you have been doing? What were you inspired to become?"

"Nothing. I would have been the same. Who knows at that time what you will become?"

"Oh! So you mean to say you don't have any aspiration. You don't have a single hobby?"

"I am not sure about my aspiration; however I am sure of one thing. If I had not been a CA, I would have been a tea vendor. Aah! But as a hobby, I love to write, but you know you can't follow that as a profession as you can't make a living out it."

"Okay! But you can write now and can share it on Facebook. If it is excellent, people will like it. You can utilize this time now instead of becoming frustrated with yourself due to uncontrollable circumstances," she said.

I looked blank.

"Shants! Don't tell me you don't know about this? If you don't know this, you are really not from this world and live in an ivory tower."

"Sincerely I did not know about it. What's that?"

"Facebook is a very famous social networking site."

"But I just knew about Orkut."

"Gone are the days of Orkut. Now everybody is using this. Facebook is far better than Orkut. It also has a chatting window; you can post anything from what you feel like to your snaps or videos. You can like things that people have shared, and also you can share apps with friends. You can share the game results too and can challenge them to take the salvo and can beat them. Also, you can search for your friends from around the globe using some keywords. It even recommends your friends based on your profile inputs."

"That's really amazing."

"Yes, it is. Let me create your account on this."

"Sure"

In those days Facebook was not a blocked site. We could easily open it in office. Since we did not have work and no boss was sitting over us, it was far more convenient for us to log in from the office. Of course, Mishika was my first friend on Facebook and the second on my list was my sister-in-law, Mags, who by now had completed her engineering and was working in an IT company in Gurgaon. She used to visit Jaipur on a weekly or bi-weekly basis. As soon as she was added to my friend's list, she asked me, "*Jiju!* What is Mishika doing in your list? How come you know her? She was my classmate and friend during my school days."

"Oh, she is my colleague in office." This platform was really fantastic. My friend list was increasing at a breakneck pace and all my free time was preoccupied with Facebook as it also provided a platform for long, endless debates on politics, views, and philosophies between friends or outsiders.

One Saturday I was sitting on my couch with my laptop on my lap, surfing Facebook and waiting for Aaisha to come back from office. Suddenly, a thought came to my mind. I remembered those 15 days when I was in Jaipur, and we both were sitting on the roof of my cousin's place watching the sunset. She was sceptical about our new life and worrying that she had to leave her home. I remember her saying, "Why is it always the girls that have to leave home?" I didn't have an answer to that. I started writing and posted on Facebook:

"By now the sun had almost taken its last breath, and they started looking towards it silently, as if their destiny had gone down to take a break to get newer challenges. Birds were returning home alone, making the whole environment alive with a lot of enthusiasm. A cold winter wind started blowing and he shivered as he was unprepared for it. She came closer to feel his heat and sheltered her head close to his face so that now he could feel her hot waves of breath on his face, making him more comfortable. A little reluctantly, he wrapped his arms around her shoulder and held her tight. Her loose hair fell time and again on their faces as if reminding them of time but the peacefulness of the moment occupied them so much that they could not feel the disturbance. He simply let her hair blow. She closed her eyes and they could feel their lips were almost touching, but he didn't dare to touch them. She let the moment pass and after a few seconds, opened her eyes. By now a beautiful silence had put down its legs so firmly that they could clearly hear their hearts beat. All the birds were back. In the distance, the sun had collected all its rays within it, and moonlight lit up her face more beautifully, and stars were appearing like a twinkling clip in her hair. He didn't want to let these moments pass; however time was flying, so reluctantly, he stood up and hugged her. Now there was a flood of tears from her side, and before she broke down completely, he touched his lips to her lips and after a long silence, uttered the words, "Definitely we will have a good start in our new life. Don't be sceptical. I will make sure that you won't miss your home. Ahh! I need to have tea now." We both smiled and went downstairs."

Within minutes of sharing, I started getting likes and comments on my post. Not to mention the first like and comment were from Mishh. It was encouraging that I had started taking my hobby of writing seriously; now, every weekend I wrote something and shared it on Facebook.

Once again, my love reappeared in my life but this time in the virtual world. When I started thinking about her, how we met, how my friends helped me to reach her, about my first date and kiss, how my parents gave me a surprise, about Mishika and Megha, a story started forming in my mind. The more I thought about her, the deeper I was in love with her. I was overwhelmed by her passion, her hard work, her caring attitude to my parents and son. The more I thought about her, the greater the gratitude I felt towards her. My ordinary life started feeling like a fantastic story. I thought I should pen it down. Every weekend, I started posting one chapter of my story. I started getting an overwhelming response from my friends. The curiosity of my friends kept me motivated. Once again, I started spending time with her in the virtual world. I didn't realize that the closer I was getting to her in the virtual world, in reality, the more we started to drift apart.

31

Obsession

This online social networking platform was so addictive that I was wholly engrossed in it. I became so obsessed with Facebook that as soon as I reached home, I would open my laptop and be glued to it, searching for online people. Of course, I chatted the most with Mishh and sometimes with Mags. As usual, now I don't remember what we chatted about, but we used to chat for hours. I believe, with Mishh, it was more about her expectation from her would-be husband and her life and with Mags, what we would plan next when she was in Jaipur on weekends.

When my father in law got special passes for IPL matches, it was always Mags and I who went for it as no one else was interested. As usual, Aaisha was busy with her schedule. Mags used to take me for long driving practice sessions in the red Maruti 800 as I was learning to drive. Sometimes Mags planned for shopping (though I hated shopping but she forced me to go with her) or exploring new dining places or movies on weekends whereas working days were spent with Mishh and long chatting sessions at night.

When my driving sessions with Mags were over, it was time to buy our own car. Again, Aaisha and I were conflicted as to which car we should buy. She always wanted to have a nice big car but considering our budget and my driving experience, I didn't want to spend much on a car. Finally we settled on Maruti car. But I had promised Mishika that before I drove it home, I would drive it to her place. So, we went to her place after the *muhuratpooja* at the famous Moti Doongri temple in the city.

Her parents warmly welcomed us. There she once again performed a *pooja* and gave me a beautiful car locket with an image of Ganpati. After that, Mishika played with my son while Aaisha and I spoke to her parents.

Again the discussion veered to finding a suitable groom for her, and her father was explaining how he had explored their entire society but had still not been able to find a good fit. Suddenly her mother cut him short and asked him to tell me about a guy who had passed out from IIM and was working in one of the MNCs, earning very decently as he was part of the top management. But the only problem with that guy was that he was half bald. Her mother knew very well that I was her best friend and hoped that I would be able to convince Mishika. I assured them that I would talk to her. Although Aaisha and I both felt that they themselves were not convinced and seemed to be in a fix.

When we were on our way back home, Aaisha started a conversation out of nowhere, "Was that Mishika whom you were talking the other night?"

I was initially stunned but then I gathered myself and replied, "Are you checking on me behind my back?"

"No! Not really." she replied. She did not pursue the topic further. But what I did not realize was that the clouds of doubts had already started hovering.

Thankfully, the weather had started turning and it had turned chill. Mishh and I had come out for a tea break in the evening. Though it was just 7 PM it was dark outside and we were sitting in a small garden.

I thought of checking with Mishh about the IIM guy as per my promise to her parents. I initiated the conversation.

"Mishh! What happened to that IIM guy?" I said casually.

"Who told you about him?" She was a bit shocked to hear about him.

"Despite the fact that you promised that you will not hide anything from me, still you are hiding things. But it does not mean that I won't come to know about it." I replied smiling.

"Shants! I am not sure what to say about him," she said, sounding a bit dejected.

"Why? Do you not like him?" I questioned.

"No! It's not about my liking. That guy is really good, smart and caring. I had a word with him and met with him and now we are talking now or then," she said.

"Then what is the problem? If he is nice, smart, caring and earning decently, then what is the confusion? Is his baldness the problem? If that is the problem, I don't really see it as a problem. Looks disappear as we age. Also, for God's sake, if something happens after marriage, will you call off your marriage? Who has seen the future and only God knows what is lying ahead!"

"That's right, Shants. Nobody has seen the future but how can we ignore the present? It's just not about that but also about his family, which seems to be bit orthodox. I think I would not be able to adjust. Since I have already hurt my parents, I don't want to hurt them again so I have accepted my fate, whatever it is," she said timidly.

"So it means you are not happy. You are just compromising because of your parents and since you are not happy, your parents are not convinced either. Baby it's the question of your life and you should not be making any compromises on it," I explained.

"No! It's not like that. I like that guy and he assured me that he will not allow anything to happen against my wishes and if he needs to go against his family at times, he will do that too. Where will you find that kind of a boy, who is ready to fight with his family too?"

"Now I am confused. Do you really like him or not?" I questioned but this time with a little frustration in my voice.

"I am not sure about it. I can't really say and that is why my father has not replied to them yet. He is looking for some other options too," she said

"Mishh! Now here you are not only deceiving yourself but also your parents and especially that guy too. You can't ride in two boats together. Either you like somebody or don't like them. There cannot be a middle path to it. So take your decision wisely and the earlier the better. If you delay your decision just because you are not sure, it will hurt all of you. That's all I have to say," I said firmly.

She did not reply and went into a long thoughtful phase. I did not disturb her either. After a long pause, she whispered, "Shants! Probably you are right. I will make my decision tonight."

Our discussion ended and we headed back to office.

That night she called me again and said, "Shants! I called off my relationship with him. I think I will not be able to adjust with him."

"That's like a girl. Now don't worry, be brave and don't regret. God has made someone special for you and he will appear soon in your life," I assured her.

While I was talking to her, I could see Aaisha turning sides again.

When Mags and I were tired of exploring Jaipur, Mags insisted on visiting Gurgaon and Delhi. I convinced Aaisha to take a day's leave from office and come along. That weekend, we explored Select City Walk, the largest mall in

Delhi, and Kingdom of Dreams in Gurgaon. Finally, when we were returning from Gurgaon in a Volvo bus, Aaisha asked me, "Shants! What are you up to?"

"What do you mean by that?"

"I have been observing you for the last few weeks. You don't have any time for me. Either you spend all your time in the office and at home with a laptop. In Mumbai, you did help me with household chores; however, now over here you don't even do that and why all of a sudden this plan to visit Gurgaon?"

"Good you asked that. In fact, this should be my complaint. I planned this visit for you only. We hardly spend any time together, and here you are living with my parents, and they took care of most of the work. So why should I worry about it."

"Or for Mags?"

"True and to be honest, partly for her too. I did want to spend some time with my sis-in-law. After all, she is my *aadhi gharwali*," I said, winking.

"*Kahi addhi ko puri banane ke chakkar mai to nahi ho?*" (Aren't you planning to make her a full wife?) In typical scenarios you never plan anything like this," she said, poking me.

"Yeah thinking of it, if you continue to behave like this."

She pinched me and said, "As if I want to remain like this. You don't understand; there is so much work which needs to be taken care of. Better if I leave the job."

"Then leave it. Why take so much pressure? But what will you do the entire day at home?"

"I don't know." She laid her head on my shoulder and I wrapped my arm around her, cuddling her and combing her soft hairs with my fingers. We were spending such precious time after a very long time. I found her a bit worried. She was still whispering in my ears, "I felt that nowadays you are getting obsessed with Mishh and Mags. Every relationship has its own limitations. I know you very well; to make them cheerful, you will do anything and will go to any extent."

"Do you doubt my intentions?"

"No! It's not about intention. It's about the limitation of relationships. We should not be crossing them as it might create misunderstandings and can create problems for everyone." She fell silent, and I was staring out of the window. I could see the passing trees and a large full moon in the distance, maintaining it's usual cool and calm like it wanted to say something to me.

Maybe I was getting obsessed with both of them and with my writing. Perhaps she was right. Perhaps I was falling for both of them as I had got some new meaning to my life and I was experiencing such a massive change for the first time. It was not about love; it was about the stories of life which I wanted to carve out. Maybe for the first time, I understood the real meaning of life and was becoming more and more selfish. Yes, this time again I was in love but with myself. I was in love with my aspirations and expectations. I didn't want to fell prey to a dull and mechanical life where one's entire childhood and adulthood was spent in achieving a meaningful career to make both ends meet as your parents wanted you to be like this. And then spending the rest of your life doing the same thing your parents did for you and finally, when your end is near, you will be thinking, what if I could have done something differently in my life. Maybe something we could have achieved for oneself, making it more meaningful, and just not dying. Perhaps we could have contributed something more to society. Maybe through our karma, we can become immortal like all those great men who are remembered for their contribution to this world. They must have faced the same kind of dilemma. However, they took the decision to swim against the tide. But what I did not realize at that time was that the clouds of misunderstanding had started gathering, and we could hardly do anything about it. In other words, I merely wanted to change myself whereas she had already warned me about where we were heading. Anyway, time was passing at its own pace.

32

Misunderstanding

Finally, the period of exile was over in the office. Our management kept its word and did not put our careers in jeopardy. As promised, they promoted me too and settled us in a new business management division as per our qualifications. Thankfully my new Vice President was well versed with my abilities. He knew how to channelize them more effectively.

He was guiding me appropriately and putting me through challenging tasks and challenging clients. I was passing all the acid tests with flying colours. It was as if, after that exile, my ability had increased substantially, and everything seemed to be so exciting in office after a long, wearisome phase. Every other month, I was being awarded a star. Every other month I was setting my own benchmarks of success, and I was surpassing them.

This resulted in more time spent in my office. Whatever time I had left, I continued to remain stuck to my laptop at home, writing something; posting on Facebook and then waiting for likes and comments. Even on weekends,

I hardly came out of the room. Either I was sleeping or busy with my laptop, chit-chatting. I was in denial mode and started ignoring Aaisha. Whatever she asked me to do, I just said no to her. I was utterly lost in my own world and stopped socializing with the outer world except for office.

During weekdays, our interactions were negligible but whatever interactions we'd had on weekends, even that had stopped, which was making her frustrated. Her frustrations kept piling up over time, waiting for some boiling point to burst.

Finally, the most memorable day of my life came. It was 9 PM. Our Vice President came rushing to my manager (who had recently joined) and said, "Shants! Something very urgent came in. We cannot push it anyway as it was requested by the management board. We need to provide some sort of explanations for numbers and it is required at the bank level and not just for one product. It is required by the day after tomorrow for a meeting. But our Operations Head wants to look at something by tomorrow so that he can prepare for the meeting. I know it's not possible but let's try to prepare something at a very high level so that at least we can give something."

Deep down in my heart, I was thinking, "Due to an inefficient data system, the absence of standard procedure and since every division was working in its own indigenous way, it took us weeks to consolidate and explain the variances to stakeholders. Despite that, every time we were defeated, as the stakeholders never seemed to be satisfied with our analysis. Now it is being asked in a day and that too based on the latest figures. How the hell will we be able to do it in just one night?"

Somehow our VP was able to read my thoughts and tried to comfort me, "Don't worry, we will use last month's data and comments only as a base and try to build something. Don't be stressed out. You just start pulling data, but I am sure you will prepare something and let's sit in the morning." He left, putting the entire burden on our shoulders.

My manager and I were looking at each other curiously, thinking about what we were going to do next. She understood my dilemma and knowing that she wouldn't be able to help much but just to comfort me, she said, "Let's go for a quick tea break and release all the stress and then we will think about how to do it."

I don't know what worked that night. Maybe it was blessings from Ma Saraswati due to Aaisha's prayers at the time of the annual event, but my mind started working clearly. Automatically, thoughts began flowing in, and I developed a framework that devised all the reasons up to the lowest level.

At midnight, my VP called me to know the status. I told him, "Sir, all done. I'm preparing to leave."

"What?" he said, astonished.

"Yes, sir. No worries! All is done. Tomorrow we just need to update the comments, and I prepared it up to the lowest level. Let them ask any question, we will be able to answer it."

He was still astounded but considering my confidence, he just said, "Okay, let's talk first thing in the morning."

In the morning, when he saw the model, he just said, "Shants! You do not realize what you have just invented. It will do wonders for you."

Since it was being discussed in the management board meeting, my VP marketed it so well and ensured that the invention did not go unnoticed at any level. It resulted in my name being nominated for 'Employee of the Year' award and the selection process for the final round kicked off. My management team kept promoting my idea to ensure that it got selected in the final round too.

One such beautiful night, just an hour before the logout time, a splendid mail came in one week before the annual grand event announcing that I had been selected for the 'Employee of the Year' award.

I gleefully reached out to my VP. He called everyone and announced on the floor, "Guys! I have amazing news for our department which will fill you with pride. This year's Employee of the Year award has been selected from our department, and it is none other than Shantilal." Everybody came to me, congratulating me. I said to my VP, "This would not have been possible without you."

"No it's all because of you, so enjoy the moment."

I immediately called Aaisha to give her the exciting news. She was so excited that she started crying and then she composed herself and just said, "This too shall pass…" and cut the line.

I didn't understand her reaction, but at that moment, I didn't give much thought to it.

One Day before the Grand Event

The event was on Sunday. I was sitting leisurely with my laptop on the sofa, surfing Facebook. Aaisha came and announced, "We are leaving in another 15 minutes to my parents' place, and you are coming with me. If I go alone, they will ask thousands of questions about why you have not come, and every time I cannot make damn excuses. It's been a long time since you visited my parent's place; I have not said anything to you."

"Okay! That's fine. I will be ready in five minutes. After all, this weekend is a grand weekend for me and it's time to celebrate."

I was about to shut down the laptop when a message from Mishh popped up on Messenger:

"Shants!!"

"Yeah, Mishh. What happened?"

"As I told you today, I am going to see him. I am very nervous." She'd told me yesterday that her father had set another date for her. The guy was a qualified Chartered Accountant and had started his own practice in Jaipur after leaving a job in Dubai.

"Why nervous? Enjoy your officially arranged date? ☺"

"Shants! Stop cracking your useless jokes. I already have so many doubts."

"Where are you?"

"Just waiting for him in CCD and talking to you."

"Are you crazy? Be cool and calm and enjoy the moment."

"I know that. Don't lecture me?"

"Then why did you ping me? Am I a time pass thing or what?"

"Shants! Don't say that? You know it well, what you mean to me. It's just that I am very anxious and not sure that this will fructify or not. I am tired of all these stupid date dramas, talking with fake smiles and if you like him, then keep waiting for their fucking answers but you know I can't do much about it. Why can't my love life be like yours?"

At that time, I didn't realize that my love life was going to be in jeopardy.

"Shants! Are you ready? We are going to leave now," Aaisha cried from outside.

"Just give me five more minutes. I am in the middle of something," I said.

"You are always in the middle of something." She sounded angry.

"Shants…"

"Shants…"

"You there?" Messages from Mishh kept popping up.

"Yes, I am here, baby. Hasn't he arrived yet?"

"Not yet. See, I told you these groom's side always think that they have the upper hand over the bride's side. Why can't they fucking come on time?"

"Oh hello… you are abusing the one who might be your life partner."

"Life partner! My foot! I am going to reject him right away. He can't bloody respect my time, then what kind of partner will he be?"

"Where are your parents?"

"They are standing outside and waiting for his family to arrive."

I was so engrossed in chatting with Mishh that I didn't realize that Aaisha was standing just behind me and giving me dirty looks.

"So this is your middle of something. If you like Mishh so much, then why don't you marry her?" she cried.

"Aaisha! What the hell are you are saying? Mind your words. She was a bit anxious and if she is getting comforted by chatting with me, what is wrong in that?"

"Yeah! It's only me who is wrong. You keep chatting. I am leaving now."

"Okay… Okay… just give me five more minutes, please. I will come along. After all, it's been a long time since I met with my second girlfriend, Mags," I said pleadingly but at the same time teasing her.

But she did not react and went outside. I assumed she would be waiting for me.

"Shants…"

"Shants…"

"Shants…"

"You there?" It was Mishh.

"Yeah! I am very much here. Hasn't he arrived yet?"

"I think he has come along with his family. I can see my parents talking to them"

"Okay! How does he look?"

"He is smart and looks dashing but a bit heavily built and quite healthy for me."

"Look who is saying! *Kallo Billo* you too are no less?"

"Shants… what do you mean by that? You mean I am MOTI."

"Nothing! See how excited you are getting."

"It seems they are coming in now."

"Okay. You focus there now. I too have to go now. Aaisha is waiting outside for so long."

"Thanks, Shants!!"

"Thanks for what?"

"Aiwahii…"

"Now you focus on him. I have to go now."

But by that time, Aaisha had already left along with Shreyansh. That night when she returned, she didn't speak a single word. I tried to placate her in many ways, but she did not budge and locked herself in the room. I thought she was angry and would be fine by morning. After all, she was my love and couldn't remain aggrieved for a long time. But what I did not realize was that yesterday's event had made her reach boiling point.

The Day of the Grand Event

It was late in the morning. She was not yet out of her room. I knocked on the door, and she did not respond.

"Look, Aaisha! I am really sorry for yesterday," I pleaded "Now please come out. It won't happen again."

She came out but didn't respond and got busy with household chores and did not speak a single word. I tried to please her, I pleaded with her, but all my efforts went down the drain.

Finally, I said, "*Yaar*, it's our grand day today when I am going to get the prestigious award of my life. Please don't be annoyed now. I will make sure that you will not be irritated anymore because of me." And that was the time she blasted me.

"Shants! It's not our grand event but only yours, and take along your Mishh or whomsoever you want with you but not me. Where am I nowadays in your life? Either it's you or your Facebook or your writing or Mishh or Mags or anything else. Where do I fit in all these? You didn't even realize what I am going through? My parents always ask why you didn't come along with me. Is something wrong between both of us and every time I give them all those damn excuses, which they are tired of hearing, but actually something is going horribly wrong with our lives and I think now is the time we should part ways. You remain happy in your life in whatever way you want, but please leave me now. I am fed up."

"Aaisha! What are you saying? I know I was wrong yesterday but why are you so angry? I told you Mishh was a bit anxious and I was trying to calm her."

"Why don't you do one thing? You marry her and always comfort her in whatever way you want."

"*AAISHA…*" I yelled angrily at her. "That's enough now."

"Don't squawk. Are you afraid of the truth or what? I warned you that you are crossing your limits; however, you didn't stop. What do you think; I can't see or hear what is going on? First, you hang out with her the whole time in office and after that, you keep chatting with her the whole night. Also, anybody can guess from your Facebook posts and stories, what is happening in your life? Who do you think you are fooling? Forget me; you don't even spend time with Shreyansh. Isn't he your son or not?"

"Aaisha! You are crossing your limit now," I said, disgusted.

"Wow! Now I am crossing the limit when you can't even hear the truth."

"Dear! She is like my sister and my best friend."

"Shants! Who the hell talks to sisters like this in this world? Best friend, my foot. Admit that you are in love with her," she roared.

"Enough is enough. You have already spoken a lot. I kept my silence; it does not mean you will say anything and I will take all that shit. I tried to make you understand many times and I even regretted my wrongdoings, but you are not stopping. What do you want from me? Can't I live my life according to my way? Why do I need to visit your parent's place every weekend? If you want to go, I never stopped you. I do have some choices in my life, and I want to fulfil them before I die." My face turned red.

"I know; what choice do you have?" Every word she uttered was filled with hatred.

"AAAISHHAAA......................" And I raised my hand on her. Every part of my body was shaking, and I broke into a sweat.

"What else can you do? You coward! I will not live with you anymore." She slammed the doors of the room on me and didn't come out until I left for my grand event. I too didn't try to console her anymore.

At the Grand Event

It was the month of December and supposed to be the coldest month of the year, and it was. But due to the morning incident, hardly any excitement was left within me for the grand ceremony. The theme was the Seven Wonders and the stage was so captivating.

I just wanted to get itover with quickly and, my heart wanted to cry aloud. My eyes were filled with tears and, I was unable to stop them. I had imagined that when I took the award in my hand, I would dedicate it to my love and even say a small speech for her, that it was possible only because of her. But now, everything looked so insipid and weary that I didn't want to stay there anymore.

Suddenly I felt a drop on my face. I thought I had started crying unknowingly. I swept away the tear from my handkerchief and tried to console myself. But then I felt another drop. Initially, I was not able to understand what was happening but when I saw everyone was running for cover, I realized it had started raining. It was raining cats and dogs. Everything was washed away. All the management which was done for the grand event went down the drain. I felt that even God was feeling the heat of her rage that he also started crying out of shock.

That day, I drank like a fish. After that, I don't know what happened next. When I took the award, what I ate and who dropped me home, I didn't remember anything. But what I realized was that all my dreams had been swept away.

A Day after the Grand Event

It was Monday morning, which was 31st December, and the last day of the year. The start of the day was very blurry to me. My mind was still under the influence of alcohol. Though it was the last day of the year, we did not have any work in the office. Just to kill time, I decided to go to the office. As expected, Aaisha did not utter a single word and neither did I, nor did I try to apologize once again. I left for office after having breakfast and picking up lunch from the dining table, which was always ready first thing in the morning by the time I woke up. The only difference from a typical normal day was that we left without talking to each other. She had taken one set of keys along with her. Thankfully, when that unfortunate incident took place, my parents had not been at home. They had gone to visit one of my maternal uncles. I was wondering if they had been at home, what they would have thought about me. They would have been very hurt. Later on, on the same day, they left for Bharatpur after I went to the office, taking another set of house keys along with them.

Epilogue

It was freezing cold, and I was tired of counting stars. Suddenly, the sky was ablaze with fireworks, which made me realize that New Year had knocked on the door. At a distance, I could hear people partying and dancing to loud music, but my heart was distressed. My eyes were red and puffed.

Once again, I saw the light of a car. This time I ignored it. Then I heard somebody calling my name downstairs. It seemed to be Aaisha, but I did not pay any attention presuming that it was just my wild imagination.

But the voice started coming closer to me. I couldn't believe it. For a few more minutes, l lay on the cot. I was not able to move my body as it was frozen due to the cold. I was just whispering, "Aaisha! Please come back. At least give me a chance to explain. I promise I will stop writing and never surf Facebook in my life again."

"Shants! Where are you?" The voice was much louder this time. I felt a ray of hope. Reluctantly, I made an effort to move my body and propped up on the railing of the roof and looked downstairs. "Aaisha! Is that you?"

"Yes, Shants! What are you doing upstairs on this freezing cold night?"

Once again, I gathered all my energy and ran downstairs and caught hold of her. I abruptly hugged her tightly in my arms and said, "Never ever do such a thing again tome. I was almost dead today." Before I could utter any more words, she placed her soft fingers on my lips and embraced me tightly.

"I am sorry," she whispered in my ears and I was about to kiss her when I heard somebody clearing her throat, "Ahem Ahem…"

I looked in the direction of the sound, and I saw Mags and Mishh entering from the main gate with a box in their hand.

"What are you both doing at this eleventh hour? And Mishh, how come your father allowed you to go out in the middle of the night and what happened to that guy? And Mags, you have not returned to Gurgaon?" I bombarded them with questions.

"Shants! Relax, why do you always ask so many questions? My father gave me permission because this time Aaisha persuaded him and look, I got engaged." She showed me her sparkling diamond ring.

"Wow!! Congratulations."

"Happy birthday, *Jiju*," Mags trumpeted. All three echoed together once again, "Happy birthday, Shants!"

"Wow! What a surprise gift when I was almost dead but wait a minute, how come you three came together?"

"What do you think, only you can tease me? Haven't I any right to tease you?" Aaisha chuckled.

"What do you mean?"

"Shants! I am really sorry that because of me you both squabbled, but you should not have raised your hand on Aaisha. It was good that Mags called me and I explained everything to Aaisha and since it was your birthday, we made this plan to tease and surprise you."

"Which was almost killing me? And what about that divorce notice?" I almost shrieked.

"What divorce notice?" Aaisha exclaimed.

"Wait a minute. Let me show you the notice which you sent me." When I looked at the envelope again, I found that it was supposed to have been delivered to house number 128 instead of 120. The postman had mistakenly dropped it at our house. I just opened it without noticing the address and saw the first line and didn't bother to read further.

"Hey, I am sorry for all the misunderstandings. Please forgive me, and I promise that it will never happen in the future again," Aaisha said remorsefully.

"But you should have picked up the phone at least or messaged me."

"Then how would it have been a surprise, my dear *jiju*?" Mags asked, grinning.

Finally, all the misunderstandings were washed away. Mishh got married after two months, and Mags too found her life partner in another six months. They both were happily married and became busy with their lives. I said goodbye to the virtual world and hence to my passion for writing. After six months, our process was again consolidated, in Pune, and this time I graciously accepted the offer to shift, just for a change. After all, this phase of our existence had passed, and we were ready to face new challenges in our new exciting life in Pune.

The Present

"That was quite a story, Shants! Why don't you write it?" Prerana asked enthusiastically.

"I think you should," Shikha too said encouragingly.

"I will when the right time comes and when Aaisha permits me as she is the one who is going to tolerate me the most when I dedicate myself to writing. All of my spare time is going to be spent on it. She is never going to allow it to happen again. I think now I am done with it." I smiled back.

After a Few Days

One day, Aaisha was working on the laptop when she found my incomplete novel and started reading it. I don't know what inspired her and she said to me, "Shants! Why don't you finish your novel?"

"Look who is saying this! Have you forgotten all those days in Jaipur?" I said mockingly.

"Shants! I am already sorry for that. Now I want you to finish your novel. I know it's one of the objectives of your life and I want you to tick it off from your checklist. I don't want you to feel remorse for it later on. I don't want you to blame me and say that because of me you were not able to complete it."

"Remember that you have to tolerate me. It means that I will not be able to accompany you anywhere for at least three months as I will be engrossed in it."

"Okay! Just three months and not more than that."

I just smiled in return, and here it is after three months ☺

The End (A New Beginning)

Acknowledgements

As rightly said, this whole world is a theatre, and everybody is playing his/her role in a story written by God. Every life he has created has some meaning and, we are so well interlinked with each other that sometimes we never realize it. Every incident in life has a meaning, however small it appears. We learn something from every incident and, nourish each of them as a part of our dreams.

So it is time to acknowledge the efforts of every person who was and is part of my journey. Without them, this dream would not have come true.

So first of all, there is no way you can thank your parents (including in-laws as they have entrusted and handed over their most beautiful gift from God to me), as without, their blessings, you are nothing.

I would like to thank my flatmates, my family from other mothers of C-402 - Kamal, Abhishek, Aasis (sorry if I have spelt it wrong. I know you were always fussy about the spelling of your name) Rathi *Sahib*, (I still can't remember his original name) Sarban and last but not the least, Rajiv and Satya, who helped me a lot in shaping and editing this entire novel.

I would like to thank my current colleagues, managers and my mentors (sorry for not mentioning your names as the list would be too long and I don't want to miss anybody ☺)in office who pushed me to complete my story when I started sharing it on our WhatsApp group. Whenever I tried to procrastinate, they would ask me where the next chapters were. And of course, my previous colleagues who were part of my journey. (Sorry boss, somebody has to play a villainous role ☺)

My special thanks to my mentors - Arvind uncle, Viresh uncle and my teachers, (especially Lalit Magazine), who shaped my life. To my love - Charu, my son, Shreyas, and my whole family who bore with me the most during this whole process.

Enough of names because everyone who is connected to me by any means is precious to me and they all deserve a big thanks. Now, to the most important and special people, the readers, a warm thanks to all of you, for investing your time in reading this and becoming an integral part of my life.

Thanks to the whole team at Notion Press for discussing and answering my crazy questions.

And last but not least; this whole story cannot be completed if I don't take these two special names with whom I cherish very special time and memories. I fought with them like anything, loved them, lived and behaved with them like a child and they inspired me and helped me in identifying this long hidden wish within me to write a story with which now I feel complete - my lovely sister in law, Megha, and my dearest friend, Ritu Pareek.

Spread love, be loved.

www.ingramcontent.com/pod-product-compliance
Lightning Source LLC
Chambersburg PA
CBHW022143050726
47590CB00002B/557